DAMEON GIBBS

Rise of the Phoenix

Act 2

To our beloved friends and family.

In order to rise from the ashes, a Phoenix, first, must burn.....

Chapter 1

June 30, 2015
  07:13 am EST

Tucker stirred awake the next morning to see Edge sprawled in an office chair, engrossed in an electronic tablet with his feet resting unceremoniously beside Tucker's head. The cramped space wasn't a luxury suite, but it served its purpose. A smirk tugged at Tucker's lips as the room's bare decor echoed his own home: stark and minimalistic. He attempted to sit up, but halfway there, his body protested, a wave of discomfort flooding him as every bruise from the previous day reminded him of its presence.

"Ugh!" Tucker exclaimed as he rolled over, placing his feet firmly on the floor.

"Morning, bright eyes. How are you feeling?" Edge called out, glancing over at the cot where Tucker lay, who merely grunted in reply.

Tucker winced as an unexpected series of pops echoed through his joints, each one a sharp reminder of yesterday's chaos. His brow furrowed, and he grimaced, feeling the unfamiliar stiffness in his shoulders and knees. It was as if his body had become a creaky old door, protesting against movement after a long period of neglect.

"I get why you think staying at a hotel could set us up for another ambush," Tucker started, "but right now, I'm convinced that the comfort of a real bed would have justified the risk over these cardboard cots."

"I told you to take some painkillers and stretch," Edge chided, his tone light and somehow rejuvenated. "But no, you had to waste time hunting for evidence before finally allowing yourself to rest." He sprang to his feet, the sudden motion earning a glare from the groggy analyst still trying to shake off sleep. "Come on, you need to get that blood pumping; let me give you a hand."

"No, I'm good. Seriously," Tucker insisted, wary that Edge's well-meaning efforts would only complicate matters further.

Without waiting for Tucker's protests, Edge pulled Tucker to his feet. The sudden motion jolted through Tucker's aching body, sending a jolt of discomfort radiating from his stiff joints.

"AHHHH, damn it!" Tucker shouted as another wave of pain coursed through him. He took a moment to breathe, allowing the discomfort to ebb before adding, "Since I'm on my feet, I might as well clean up. Where's the shower?"

Edge gestured toward the door, chuckling as Tucker hobbled past him like a wounded giant. Both men had barely managed four hours of sleep, having spent the night meticulously collecting evidence from the vehicle and gear of the fallen soldiers at the cabin before navigating the nearly impassable, mud-slicked road.

Like the John Doe entangled in quicksand, they found themselves stumped, unable to establish any definitive identities for the bodies. The car, weapons, and the distinctive armor seemed to have no traceable links to any supplier or military base. It felt as though all the clues had simply evaporated into thin air.

Tucker scoured multiple databases, tapping into resources from the CIA, the military, and even MI-6. Regrettably, his searches yielded no results.

"We have billions of dollars at our disposal across countless agencies, and we can't even find a driver's license," Edge thought as he thumbed through the headlines.

Agents Reid and Webster stepped through the door, their faces a mix of determination and fatigue. Reid's eyes flickered with a hint of eagerness, while Dana wore the weariness of too many sleepless nights etched into his features. Edge, leaning against the wall with an ease born from countless late nights, nodded in acknowledgment, his posture relaxed despite the tension in the air.

Tucker, however, was a different story. Dark circles shadowed his eyes, and his brow was creased with the weight of exhaustion. He rubbed the back of his neck as if trying to massage away the fatigue that clung to him like a damp blanket. Each slow blink of his eyelids revealed just how hard he was fighting to stay alert, the remnants of yesterday's chaos still lingering in his mind. The contrast between Edge's composed demeanor and Tucker's struggle was stark, highlighting the toll the relentless pace had taken on him.

"I need him to be on top of his game. The man runs like a computer, but without rest he's bound to make mistakes; mistakes that may take us down the wrong path," Edge thought as he wondered about what the big man did to distract himself. *"When this is over, I'm taking him on a hiking...though a strip club might do him more good."*

Tucker emerged from the shower, his pace quickened and a hint of refreshment coursing through him. Yet, the memories of yesterday clung to him like a shadow. As the water cascaded over him, he could almost feel Wolf's knife, its cold edge pressed against his throat. He had hoped the anxiety would fade, but deep down, he knew his mind would replay those harrowing moments, especially the image of Bull taking his own life. Glancing at Edge, he noted the man's calm demeanor, even after the chaos of battle. Tucker recognized that Edge was a seasoned soldier, but how could anyone be so composed after ending seven lives without a flicker of emotion? He appeared unchanged from the day they first crossed paths.

"No real change in his facial expression, no signs of worry or soreness, let alone any indication of stress," Tucker mused, a mix of admiration and disbelief washing over him. He went to say something when a knock came at the door, followed by Reid's entrance.

"Morning, team," Reid announced, stepping into the room. He placed a laptop on one of the tables, sliding it toward Tucker and Edge. "They've wrapped up the analysis on Arslan's video."

Tucker raised an eyebrow in disbelief. "I was under the impression the techs needed until later this afternoon to finish."

At the first screening of Arslan's video, the outcome fell far short of expectations. The glare from the sun and reflections on the glass rendered everyone but Nezaket a mere shadowy figure. Compounding the issue, the audio was so faint that the chirping of birds overhead completely overshadowed any potential evidence that could be discerned.

Reid sighed, a knowing look in his eyes. "I'm familiar with the guy you talked to. He has a tendency to act like a hero after he resolves things quickly. Sure, it took him a while to figure it out, but deep down, he was aware it would take less time than he initially claimed."

"Well, I hope we got something good," Tucker said as he nodded towards the laptop.

"Before we play it, let me preface by saying he got us something," Reid told them.

Edge sat down next to Reid. "What do you mean 'something'?"

"He managed to separate the audio tracks, allowing us to catch snippets of the conversation—provided we crank the volume all the way up. We ran the voices through our audio databases, but came up empty; not even a trace of Gamze," Reid explained.

Reid started the video which showed some of the Everglades. He continued to narrate the video, "The beginning is just Arslan running through the 'Glades." He hit the fast forward button causing the video to squeal as the footage sped up before he stopped at a scene showing the cabin. "Okay, here's where he started recording the meeting between his father and our mystery men.

"As you can see there was little, they could do to clear up the picture," Reid said as he attempted to adjust the video on the laptop.

Despite the unsteady camera angle capturing the meeting room, the silhouettes of those present were discernible, though insufficiently clear for positive identification. The exception was Gamze, who occupied the head of the table, flanked by his bodyguards, their arms crossed over their belts in a display of vigilance. Positioned at the opposite end, another man faced away from the camera, leaving only his bald head visible—a detail that offered little to aid in their search for leads.

Turning the volume up, they could finally discern the exchange between Gamze and the unidentified figure.

"*Are the plans in motion?*" the bald man asked.

"*Of course, they are,*" Gamze responded with a hint of pride in his voice. "*And as long as you hold up your end of the plan, things should continue to go smoothly, and honor will be restored to my country by the end of it.*"

"*We have much more than the honor of your country riding on this, and yes, many great things are going to happen. The restoration of a forgotten dissolved empire is not a priority.*"

Nezaket's body language transformed, and even through the distorted video, his fury radiated like a crimson halo.

"*This is about hitting Global Trust and establishing the Order,*" The faceless man lectured Nezaket.

"*What are you talking about?*" Gamze inquired, his irritation palpable. "*It has been promised to me that the Kilij would get your resources and enhance our reputation! Without me the Order would be nothing; without my resources this operation would be a rock in a pond and simply sink without a ripple!*"

The man stood and crossed the room, his footsteps echoing against the wooden floor, as he settled into a chair next to Gamze.

"*You will get to claim victory but not the way you want it. You'll get the bulls-eye on your back and no support from us. You'll simply be the scapegoat that allows the Order to move onto the next stage unnoticed,*" the man said.

"*You wouldn't dare dishonor me in such a way!*" Gamze lashed. "*If so, you will bring hell down upon yourself!*"

The man let out a low laugh at the threat. "*Ah, my old friend... I dwell in hell itself, and when necessary, I serve as its herald. The tides are shifting, and our reliance on you has reached its end.*"

Gamze's fury ignited as he slammed his fist onto the table, the wood vibrating under the force of his anger. He rose to his full height, eyes blazing with indignation. In a seamless motion, the bald man followed suit, his hand reached for his weapon and pressed the barrel against Nezaket's head. A deafening bang shattered the silence, echoing through the cabin as Arslan instinctively ducked from sight, heart racing, leaving only the haunting sounds of gunfire reverberating.

"Well, that was brutal," Reid commented.

"And efficient," Edge added. "It was planned. The killer set up his men, so they had the tactical advantage. Did you see the signal he gave?" Reid and Tucker shook their head. "When he sat down on the table his men made a slight adjustment. As soon as Gamze was executed, they jumped into action."

"Well, this confirms that Gamze and his men knew their attackers. Otherwise, they wouldn't have let their guard down like that," Reid commented. "Also, did I hear that guy right: the 'Order'? Is this a religious cult?"

"I'm not sure," Tucker responded as he went to his folders. "I don't recall hearing any whispers about an organization by that name." He sifted through his files, examining the scattered sheets of paper.

"You probably won't catch wind of it either," Reid cautioned. "It seems like they've been putting in a lot of effort to remain under the radar, employing various fronts to mask their activities. Plus, 'the Order' could stand for something else," he added.

Tucker dropped one of the folders on his bed. "You don't get involved with a man like Nezaket without having credibility. Which means this 'Order' had to have done something to establish itself in the world."

Edge sat, still looking at the laptop, scratching his chin. "What if... perhaps their efforts to establish themselves were confined to the US and didn't extend abroad?"

"Then we definitely would've known about it," Reid said leaning back in his chair.

"Not if they're working with the government," Edge advised.

Tucker stepped back from the laptop, disbelief etched across his face. "Given what happened yesterday, I'm convinced someone's keeping tabs on us. This video indicates there's an organization with enough influence to impress Gamze. But I refuse to believe a government agency is in league with them. My instincts tell me this is part of an assault on the US, and I can't fathom any government backing that. We need to dig deeper; I'm confident we'll uncover who they are or at least identify their associates as a starting point."

"They may be affiliated with a government agency under false purposes," Edge suggested. "And the government doesn't understand their real agenda. Think – how many missions have you heard about where former special operation types used our government's resources to establish their criminal enterprise? Heck, I once killed a former US Marshall that was involved in human trafficking in Europe."

Tucker stroked his head as he walked back towards the table. "Arslan mentioned that Gamze wanted him to witness something, didn't he? A specific event. Reid, are you certain your team didn't uncover any leads on a potential terrorist target?"

"Nothing of symbolic importance," Reid said. "It's just a bunch of mundane events coming up: baseball games, races, carnivals."

"Then how about this Global Trust place? What you know about it?" Edge asked and turned his attention to Reid, who was now deep in thought.

With the room silent, Reid took a moment before he snapped his fingers. "It's a major international bank located in Miami, one of the city's landmarks being the tallest towers."

"What specifically do they deal with?" Edge asked.

Reid shrugged. "I think large companies like oil or mining. But I'll grab Crawford and get a better picture."

Pete Crawford rounded out Reid's tight-knit team. He had just returned from a vacation in Sweden, summoned back specifically for this case. Arriving the previous night, he looked as haggard as Tucker and Edge after their grueling excursion in the 'Glades. The effects of time zone shifts, and lengthy layovers had left him resembling a zombie.

"You think he's over his jet lag yet," Edge asked.

"Just put six cups of coffee in him and he'll be ready to go. Anyway, I'll get a list of Global Trust's clients and any new ventures they're getting involved with," Reid continued.

"I wouldn't expect a major bank like that to give you that information willingly," Edge warned.

"I don't expect them to either, but I know some people that can get us that information on them via other less official routes," Reid tapped the table sharply before exiting the room.

Edge stood up and pressed play on the video again. He watched the scene of Gamze's head snapping back, the red mist covering his men. "*No kid should have to watch their father's murder.*"

Tucker watched as Edge focused on the execution. "What's on your mind?"

"Can you imagine having to witness something like this at that kid's age?" Edge answered.

Tucker studied him for a beat before he replied, "It's tragic, but there's something else on your mind."

Edge closed the laptop and walked over to Tucker. "It doesn't bother you that those guys knew exactly where to find us at the cabin? Or how they knew so much about us?"

"I think it's obvious, they somehow tapped our phones," Tucker paused to think. "Do you think they've infiltrated our group?"

"I wouldn't shoot the idea of a mole down, especially after yesterday. I mean, how did they know to tap *our* phones? No one knows the reason we're down here except for a small number of people and only a few of them know us by name," Edge said.

Tucker shook his head. "Look Edge, the people involved with any aspect of this case has all been thoroughly vetted."

"Do you remember the Cold War? Don't you think there are spies who'd gotten past the vetting process? Groups like this plan years in advance and slowly infiltrate people into key positions," Edge responded with a hint of frustration.

Tucker remained skeptical of Edge's conspiracy theory. While past events supported Edge's assertions, they didn't fit the current situation. "I agree, we might have underestimated their access to certain resources, but that just means they're well financed. Somehow, they can get the top-of-the-line technology, allowing them to tap our communications or intercept e-mails. And on top of that, hire the mercenaries we encountered."

"Mercs? You think those were mercs?" Edge interrupted. "Those were not mercs. I've fought mercs and have worked with them. They get *paid* to do a job, but they don't inject *potassium cyanide* from a wristband into their body to prevent themselves from talking. These guys are way above and beyond hired mercenaries on the commitment scale. This 'Order' is more than a bunch of soldiers of fortune; it requires cult-like devotion from its members. And if this group can sneak Gamze into the country, and then can afford to kill him, they have the ability to infiltrate the government and monitor this case."

Tucker couldn't help but chuckle internally. Countless times he had stood before his superiors, laying out his case with solid facts and thumping the table for emphasis. Now, he found himself on the opposite side of the debate. Edge's expression revealed that he was no longer considering this a mere theory. With each new fragment of evidence, the conspiracy was taking on a more tangible form for him.

"Then who do we look at?" Tucker questioned. "Reid? Webster? The shrinks? What about all the techs that worked the crime scene? Or that coroner, Dr. Bailey? How about Crawford, huh? He wasn't even in the country until last night. Is he a suspect, too? Who do we investigate?"

Tucker felt a surge of irritation at Edge's skepticism toward the government, a sentiment he chalked up to the usual disdain Delta operatives had for intelligence agents. Nevertheless, he chose to entertain Edge's line of thinking and ride the wave of his speculation.

Edge took a deep sigh. "With the window we have, we won't be able to find the mole. Especially, once we head to Global Trust."

"You wanna head out before Reid gets us the information?" Tucker said.

"Hell no. Before we go, I'm looking over the blueprints for that building."

"What are you hoping to get out of that?" Tucker asked.

Edge walked to gaze out the room's window, "The Order hasn't hit Global Trust yet but I'm sure they're going to hit it soon, and we'll need to be there when they do. But I'm not walking into another trap. I want to know all our available paths and possible choke points. It's harder to adapt in a building than in the woods."

"What do you mean by *we*?" Tucker said, taking a step closer.

"This case is changing fast. It's clear you won't be able to sit on the sidelines." Edge's tone made Tucker feel like he was getting one hell of a pep talk.

"I don't do this shit, Edge. I barely escaped yesterday. Without your help, I…"

"They know who you are," Edge cut him off. "They'll kill you as soon as they can get you alone and believe it or not, coming with me to stop these assholes is safer than staying here with a mole."

Tucker mused on the thought. *"That is the craziest thing I have ever heard. And yet, it makes a lot of sense. If there is a mole."*

"I'm guessing I don't have a lot of say in this matter?" Tucker eventually spoke up.

"Not in the slightest, well if you want to stay alive that is," Edge responded with a hint of a smile.

"Figures," Tucker responded. "Well, if don't think we can find the mole, can we, at least, establish who we can trust?"

"Reid and Dana are solid. I've looked into them and trust their body language. Now, we need to look into the other and get a layout on the bank. But first I need soda," Edge declared before stepping out of the room.

Tucker remained rooted to the spot, the weight of the revelation crashing over him—this case had ensnared him in a deadly game, with unseen enemies eager to end his life.

"I'm not in Kansas anymore," he thought as he followed Edge out of the room, craving something much stronger.

Chapter 2

The clock had just passed three in the afternoon when the team gathered in Reid's office. Edge was hunched over his tablet, scrutinizing the blueprints of Global Trust he had downloaded. Tucker, however, had thrown in the towel after thirty minutes, his eyes straining against the tiny text and convoluted pathways. In contrast, Edge had been engrossed in the plans for nearly two hours, his focus unwavering.

Reid stacked his notes neatly, glancing at a new text from Dana. "Agents Webster and Crawford have uncovered additional information, and she's en route. Crawford is sticking with the tech team to dig deeper."

"Let me guess, the bank refused to hand over their client list?" Edge inquired.

"Not a chance, no matter how sweetly we asked," Reid confirmed, his tone tinged with exasperation. "Even Webster put on that 'adorable phone voice' of hers, but they still wouldn't budge." He shrugged, the gesture a mix of frustration and resignation.

For a fleeting instant, Edge found himself curious about what Dana's "adorable phone voice" might sound like.

"However," Reid continued, "while they may keep their list behind closed doors, thanks to the world of public records and the Internet, those doors are a mere annoyance."

"You're saying you hacked the bank? At this point, I would have sent down a few heavily armed agents," Tucker asked, incredulous.

"Didn't have to. A bank like Global Trust leaves a digital trail that's hard to erase completely. We combed through the web for anything linking Global Trust to other companies via projects and deals, and we struck gold—hundreds of hits surfaced. It's all about knowing where to look," Reid said, a grin spreading across his face. "While it may not cover every angle, I'm confident we can piece together a solid overview of their operations from what we've dug up," he elaborated.

Tucker nodded in approval. "I like it. Now the million-dollar question: did you find anything?"

"Indeed," Reid replied, his eyes glinting with intrigue. "They have substantial ties to global mining, drilling, and oil corporations, while also overseeing various international banks as a parent entity. Numerous smaller ventures have been swallowed up through aggressive takeovers—remarkably aggressive, to be precise. They were recently scrutinized for their intimidation tactics against other banks. However, the most compelling detail is a recent agreement between Global Trust and a Turkish oil firm," Reid concluded.

"Turkish Petroleum; Gamze's company," Tucker guessed with a smile. Reid just winked in approval. "Okay, we're heading over. I want court orders; these guys can't have an ounce of wiggle room. Reid who can we call?"

"I know a few judges that I've dealt with in the past that is light on needing substantial evidence," Reid suggested.

Reid moved to his desk, rifling through a stack of dusty case files in search of the judges' contact details. Meanwhile,

Tucker scribbled notes, outlining his pitch for the judges. The process felt foreign; court orders weren't typically part of his operations.

Dana burst through the door, her breathless urgency palpable. "You need to see this!" she shouted, her eyes wide as she flicked on Reid's TV. Reid and Edge shifted their focus, but Tucker stayed locked onto his notes, the weight of the situation pressing down on him.

Edge's jaw went slack as he stared at the screen, his eyes wide with disbelief. He had witnessed horrors in some of the most devastated regions of the globe, yet nothing compared to this. Reid stood frozen, equally astonished, while Dana glanced between the two men, her expression mirroring the shock that must have spread across everyone else watching the broadcast.

"What's going on?" Tucker asked, his mind racing. It wasn't that he was indifferent; it was just that he needed to capture his thoughts on paper before they slipped away.

"Remember that event Arslan was talking about?" Edge asked.

Tucker replied absently, "Sure."

"Well, I think it just happened," Edge answered.

Tucker spun around in his chair and focused his attention on the TV. Shocked by what he saw, "Turn the volume up," he asked.

"Around 3:45 PM Eastern Standard Time, a C–130 Hercules cargo plane soared over Miami, unleashing six missiles," the reporter announced, his voice steady but laced with urgency. "The assault has wreaked havoc on Miami International Airport, forcing all air traffic to reroute to surrounding airports. The downtown Financial District has also been struck. We currently lack footage, but eyewitness accounts describe a scene engulfed in dust and smoke, with flames rapidly consuming buildings across the city. Reports indicate that a massive section of street has collapsed into a gaping crater where one missile is believed to have hit. The once-proud skyscrapers that defined Miami's skyline now lay shattered among the debris."

The reporter paused, his brow furrowing as he pressed a finger to his ear, straining to catch the voice in his earpiece. His eyes darted around the studio, reflecting the urgency of the moment, before he nodded slightly, as if confirming something crucial. The tension in his posture spoke volumes, a silent acknowledgment that the news he was about to deliver would change everything.

"Confirmation has just come in: the Turkey Point nuclear power plant has been struck, resulting in a blackout across the city. Early reports indicate that there are currently no verified radiation leaks. Civilians are being evacuated while we await an official assessment on the potential for leaks."

The reporter took a moment to let the gravity of the situation settle before continuing, "The President has issued a State of Emergency. As the city spirals into chaos, the National Guard is being deployed to the explosion sites and nearby areas, preparing for evacuation, rescue efforts, and quarantine measures..."

The reporter pressed his finger to his earpiece again, then pulled it away to announce, "Breaking news: a terrorist organization from Turkey, known as the 'Kilij,' has claimed responsibility for the attack. Details are still emerging."

Reid broke the silence, "What do we do now?"

Tucker had no idea. For the first time, he was totally lost. "I... I don't know."

Edge switched off the television, his gaze locking onto the

team. "The Kilij are just a front, a distraction. Our priority is to uncover the identity of this 'Order' and eliminate them. The destruction we've just witnessed is unimaginable, but we're here to uncover the truth, not wallow in despair. We'll grieve later—right now, we need to focus on bringing the Order to justice."

"You're damn right," replied Dana.

"Then it's decided; we ramp up our efforts, no matter the cost," Edge declared, his conviction unwavering.

The team dove into a frenzy of gathering information about the attack, scouring every news outlet available. After hours spent poring over harrowing reports, they uncovered the grim reality: thousands were feared dead, the power plant would remain offline for a minimum of two years, and power outages would plague the city for weeks to come. At ground zero, only a handful of structures still stood amidst the ruins, one of which was the now-infamous Global Trust, drawing attention like a moth to a flame.

"Son of a bitch! All this was a setup so they could go after the bank. Tucker, we need to get in there. And I mean now!" Edge exclaimed.

Tucker wasted no time voicing his thoughts. "We can't just waltz in there; we need clearance. You've seen the reports: the President has that location secured more tightly than Fort Knox." Edge shot him an impatient glance. Tucker pressed on, "Only the higher ups can grant us access."

Edge fixed his gaze on Tucker, determination etched across his features. "Then you'd better ring your boss and make this happen. We need to find a room where we can use a phone that isn't under surveillance."

"I like where you are going with this," Tucker replied, moving quickly to keep pace with Edge.

Miami's proximity meant that many agents at the Department of Homeland Security had loved ones caught in the chaos of the bombings. The empty offices, strewn with forgotten paperwork and flickering screens, bore witness to the heartache unfolding within the agency. Reid's team departed, their faces somber, heading to offer support to colleagues who were grappling with the harsh reality of confirmed losses.

Edge discovered a vacant office, belonging to a junior administrative assistant; a space devoid of critical secrets, where phone taps would be unnecessary. Tucker dialed Director Winford's office, leaving a message with the secretary that included the office number for a callback and emphasized the urgency of his request.

"If there is anyone who can get a hold of him during a crisis, it's her," Tucker thought.

Sure enough, not even two minutes later the phone rang, and Director Winford was on the line. "Hello, Director. This is Tucker."

"I know it's you, Tucker. What do you need? Time is a luxury we don't have. The President has his hand so deep in my business, he could probably pull out my tonsils," Winford replied, his tone as flat as the surface of a still lake.

"Sir, I apologize for the inconvenience, but we've come to believe that—"

"In my line of work, time equals lives son. So give me the facts. Save the pleasantries," Winford interrupted.

Tucker had heard this side of him before as it was being directed to others. "I will get straight to the point," Tucker assured him. "Gamze had his hand in the attack on Miami, but I'm afraid he wasn't working alone."

"I'm not sure I follow. You're saying that Gamze Nezaket helped orchestrate all this? Are you sure?" Winford asked.

"If not all of it, then, at least, the largest part, especially the logistics. Apparently the Kilij were providing resources to some group who call themselves the 'Order.' When Gamze had given them enough resources to execute to attack, they killed him," Tucker continued.

A tense silence hung on the line before Winford's voice cut through. "How can you be so sure? And how in the hell did Gamze get taken out in the desolate Everglades, by someone other than our team? We were supposed to track his every move, down to the minute he needed to relieve himself! Didn't I instruct you to keep this under wraps? This case is plastered across every news outlet if you haven't noticed!"

"Yes, you did, but what's being reported is misinformed information. The Kilij are being set up as the scapegoats. The Order fed the information to the news to distract attention from themselves while they took their next steps." Tucker swore he could hear the director grinding his teeth on the other end of the line. "I can crack this case if you can get me into ground zero, sir. Tonight."

"Ground Zero? That's impossible," Winford replied, his voice laced with doubt. "With all that's happened today, there's no way I can get that approved."

Edge had been tuned into Tucker's conversation, piecing together the unfolding dialogue. Tucker responded with a thumbs-down gesture.

Edge whispered forcefully, "No! We need to get in there!"

Tucker nodded, steeling himself for another attempt. "Director, we suspect the Order plans to infiltrate Global Trust International Bank tonight. Their objective seems to be compromising the security systems and funneling funds into offshore accounts that would evade our detection. This was hinted at in the video we uncovered. The bank has connections with nearly every major international oil company, including Gamze's. If they gain access, they could potentially secure limitless financial resources to sustain their operations indefinitely. Our best chance is to intercept them while local law enforcement is preoccupied with rescue efforts."

"So, you're implying that the bombing was a decoy?"

"Yes, I am," Tucker assured.

The line went quiet again before the director's voice broke through the stillness. "Do you possess any evidence to back this assertion?"

"Evidence!? Are you kidding me? After everything that just happened, you still want proof?" Tucker's mind screamed.

Tucker's mind raced, but he remained calm. "Sir, under these conditions, the courtroom-grade evidence is going to be hard to come by. The best we can do at this point is probable cause, and I think what we heard on the videotape meets that standard."

"So, you have a video of a dead terrorist, referring to a bank. For all, I know the bombing that took place today was a failed attempt by him to bomb that very bank," Winford suggested.

"Sir, I'm confident there were no errors in the targeting. The missiles aimed at the airport and the nuclear facility hit precisely where they intended to cripple operations. There was no miscalculation involved. I doubt the remaining missiles were carelessly hurled into the financial district just to cause chaos. The fact that Global Trust, which isn't exactly the largest player in that area, remains one of the few structures still intact and suggests it was spared on purpose. Considering the details we've gathered from the videotape, the coincidence is too significant to overlook!" Tucker explained.

Edge couldn't help but admire Tucker's tenacity. Many would have backed down when trying to push their perspective onto a superior, driven by a need to protect their career.

A heavy breath escaped the director, followed by a long pause. "Fine," he relented at last. "You've made your case. But I still can't grant you access to Ground Zero or provide any extra support tonight. The White House has seized all my resources. With Miami declared a disaster zone and the terrorist implications, martial law is now in effect."

"This is vital to the investigation, and I wouldn't push if it weren't," Tucker pressed, his voice steady but urgent. "If you or the President are unwilling to pursue these criminals, then deny my request for access to Ground Zero. But if you're committed to capturing them... then make sure I get into that building!"

"The earliest I can get you in is tomorrow morning," Winford asserted.

Tucker's fist slammed onto the desk, causing the picture frames of the desk's owner to fall over. "Tomorrow morning?"

"It's the earliest I can manage. Either you accept it, or you don't. No exceptions," Winford replied, irritation creeping into his tone as he struggled to contain his frustration with Tucker's relentless push.

"It will have to do," Tucker answered, clearly not understanding Winford's lack of support.

"Very well, I'll ensure you're in there first thing tomorrow. In the meantime, get some rest, and keep your plans about entering Global Trust to yourself, understood?" Winford instructed.

"Understood, sir," Tucker gritted his teeth as he slammed the handset onto the cradle, sending it bouncing off the desk and crashing to the floor along with a couple of pens and a framed photograph. "Damn it!" he cursed, his pulse quickening as confusion mingled with anger.

He couldn't fathom why access to the site was being withheld. Shaking his head, he forced himself to breathe deeply, trying to quell the storm of frustration swirling inside him. Winford had to have a reason for his obstinacy, even if it felt like a betrayal in the heat of the moment.

Edge observed Tucker's clenched fists, his voice low and urgent. "He's holding us off until tomorrow morning? You know that's unacceptable, right?"

"According to the director, all his resources are busy hunting down the terrorists so he can't give us any help and doesn't seem to think that time is of the essence in getting us there."

"He does seem a little myopic about the urgency," Edge agreed.

Tucker struggled to justify his boss's decision, despite his reservations. "Perhaps he's missing the bigger picture, but who can say what political tides are turning right now? I wouldn't want to be in his position. He's demonstrated time and again that he knows his way around this game, and he's come through for me more times than I can count."

"Why can't the Director of the CIA, who answers only to the President, get clearance?" Edge demanded, frustration lacing his voice. The walls of the cramped office felt like they were closing in on him, and he knew there was no one higher to turn to for help.

Tucker folded his arms tightly across his chest, his shoulders slumping as a heavy sigh escaped him.

"Those bastards are going to be in Global Trust tonight!" Edge insisted.

"I couldn't agree more, but I have orders to stand down 'till morning. So, what do you propose we do until then?" Tucker asked.

"Tucker, he ordered that *you* wait until tomorrow; not me or anyone else. I have vowed to protect this country from enemies foreign and domestic at all costs, and these guys are the enemy. I can't sit still for this. You remember Operation Nightwolf, right?" Edge continued.

"Sure, I do."

"I defied orders to complete that mission back then. And you know as well as I do, it's what we need to do now," Edge asserted, rising to his feet.

Tucker dragged his palms down his face, startled by the slickness of sweat coating his skin. "You expect me to defy the director?"

"I'm just pointing out what I know I have to do," Edge responded.

For the first time in his career, Tucker faced a pivotal choice: obey Winford's orders or act on his own judgment. He glanced at Edge, who was already gearing up to move forward, ready to take action whether Tucker joined him or not. In that brief moment of internal conflict, the weight of his responsibility to protect the country eclipsed any concerns he had about his career.

"I'm on board. However, we can't do this alone," Tucker insisted.

Edge smiled. "I don't think Reid's team will need much persuasion."

"Alright, let's go and debrief them," Tucker said.

Chapter 3

In a warehouse on the fringes of Miami, a cadre of men clad in cutting-edge military gear meticulously inspected their equipment, honed their blades, and finalized their explosives. Though this wasn't an official military unit, the operation mirrored the discipline of any elite Special Forces team. Each mission underwent rigorous practice and rehearsal long before the actual execution.

The warehouse floor resembled a complex maze of plywood panels and makeshift staircases, each segment meticulously designed to replicate key zones of their intended target. Though the constructions appeared rudimentary at first glance, every doorway and staircase mirrored the precise specifications of their blueprints. Elevated observation towers loomed over the mock corridors, ready to relay crucial feedback. At the heart of this arrangement lay the team's preparation zone, cluttered with tables and stacked ammunition crates, buzzing with anticipation.

A solitary figure loomed before the table, his hands locked behind him. Shadows cloaked his features, casting an air of mystery as he surveyed the assembly of lethal professionals before him. Each member of this elite cadre had proven themselves through a relentless gauntlet of trials—operational precision, tactical adaptability, and an unwavering ruthlessness were the hallmarks of their selection. In this man's world, compassion was a liability, and those who hesitated were swiftly cast aside.

"Circle up," the shadow man ordered with authority.

The soldiers halted their tasks, shifting their focus to the table. This was no egalitarian Round Table; the air crackled with a clear hierarchy. Only two men were permitted to flank the leader. To his right stood an Asian man, his stature slightly shorter than the imposing figure at the center.

Hitoshi, the unit's digital savant, possessed the uncanny ability to breach nearly any system, no matter how fortified. His notoriety soared after he infiltrated the CIA and NSA databases, jeopardizing a multitude of undercover operatives—all executed with nonchalance while he lounged in an airport terminal. His roots extended deep into the Kōga region of Japan, a secluded area shrouded in mystery and historically linked to the legendary ninja clan that bore its name. The Kōga clan's legacy stretched back to the mid-1400s, enduring through centuries by mastering the arts of stealth and survival within the rugged, hidden mountains of Japan. From his earliest steps, Hitoshi was immersed in rigorous training, honing skills in subterfuge and lethality that would make him a formidable asset in this shadowy world.

To the right of the shadowy figure towered Draggo, a hulking soldier from the Russian Special Forces. Once part of the elite Spetsnaz "Alfa" Anti-Terrorist Group, he loomed at six foot five, his hard, chiseled features carved by years of conflict. His piercing gaze held an unsettling intensity, capable of freezing anyone who dared to meet it. A battle-hardened veteran, Draggo had long since crossed moral lines, engaging in operations that left no room for the conventions of warfare.

The two lieutenants had clawed their way to their ranks through sheer grit and sacrifice, often at a personal cost. Yet, like every member of this unit, their allegiance and respect for their commander stemmed from more than just a healthy dose of intimidation. He was a leader who rewarded success but tolerated no blunders. The consequences for failure were so severe that no one repeated the same mistake—not because they learned from it, but because they didn't live to tell the tale. What intensified their trepidation was their leader's uncanny knack for being aware of everything that transpired, even in his absence.

Their leader moonlighted, in what he called his "hobby," as an accomplished spy with the CIA. He had received multiple commendations and medals for going beyond the call of duty, but his reasons for going rogue remained uncertain to most.

With his men's full attention their leader leaned into the light revealing his bald head and meticulously trimmed goatee. Keeast, the head of the Order's elite tactical "Black Unit," was not afraid to get his hands dirty. He began the mission briefing.

"Tonight, we'll touch down on the rooftop of Global Trust in a National Guard medevac chopper. Following the so-called 'tragedy' that has befallen this 'once-great city,' as only medical aircraft are permitted in the red zone." Keeast sneered, his voice dripping with sarcasm as he mimicked the sensationalist tone of the news coverage surrounding Miami's recent chaos.

"From there, we'll breach the 22nd floor through the rooftop access. Our entry point is a maintenance stairwell adjacent to the elevator shaft. Keep in mind, this is a lights-out operation. With power down across the city, Global Trust will rely solely on emergency backup generators. We'll be navigating with night vision; that's our only option."

"First, Lox will disable the security door on the rooftop. Once inside, we'll descend to the eighteenth floor, where the bank's mainframe awaits."

A soldier at the edge of the group inclined his head, a subtle gesture that spoke volumes. His eyes flickered with determination as he adjusted the grip on his weapon, ready to embrace the challenge ahead.

Keeast continued, "Everyone will proceed down to either the sixteenth or seventeenth floor, depending on your respective station, except for Hitoshi and myself. We will remain at the mainframe to complete the transfer. You will establish a perimeter on the sixteenth floor," Keeast commanded, his tone sharp and unyielding. "Position yourselves at both the north and south ends of the main hallway to secure the elevator and stairwells. Bricks and Lox, you'll remain behind to neutralize any unwelcome guests."

Keeast thumbed through the blueprints, his finger tracing the jagged lines that indicated barricades and choke points. He paused, tapping a section marked in red, the ink bold against the faded paper. Each mark signified a potential obstacle, a calculated risk that could either fortify their advance or spell disaster. The air thickened with tension as he studied the layout, his gaze sharp and focused.

"Those defensive positions will give you the upper hand against any intruders. Our intel suggests an attack is improbable, but it's better to be safe than sorry. If things go sideways, you can retreat to the seventeenth floor and regroup with the rest of the team."

Keeast jabbed his finger at the blueprint, pinpointing the

narrow corridor wedged between two elevator shafts.

"The elevators and stairwells to the right are the sole access points for any intruders attempting to reach our floor. That barricade between the elevators needs to be impenetrable! If they manage to breach our initial defense, I want them forced to navigate the lengthy route through the lawyers' offices before they can reach the elevator. Our goal is to buy ourselves time; by the time they break through, we should have the package secured and be making our exit. The remainder of the team will hold their ground on the seventeenth floor, with Draggo positioned as the final bastion against any threats. And judging by this charming blueprint, once they step onto the seventeenth floor, it'll be game over for them."

Keeast's lips curled into a smirk as his fingers glided over the marked area on the blueprint, the kill box clearly outlined in bold red ink.

"Once Hitoshi breaches the mainframe, he'll deploy a virus that will shut down all alarms, giving us the crucial time needed to finalize the transfer. Exactly forty minutes after that, the firewall will collapse, triggering the alarms and unlocking the bank's security doors while sealing off key zones and escape routes. It's vital that everyone is on the nineteenth floor or above by then; otherwise, you'll find yourselves cornered. And if you find yourself cornered... you know the protocol."

The men exchanged glances, a silent understanding passing among them. A couple of them adjusted the straps on their wrists, fingers brushing against the small capsules hidden within the sleek bracelets.

"Gentlemen, we are charting a new path for this nation and soon, the globe. We will be labeled as traitors, conspirators, and terrorists. Our homeland will never accept us back into its embrace. But that is of little consequence, for they remain unaware of the truths we hold. They cannot grasp that our actions will lay the groundwork for a new era." Keeast let a smile creep across his face as he relished the gravity of the moment.

"Miami burns, a city engulfed in flames. This is our launchpad, the birthplace of the Order of the Phoenix. From these ashes, we will forge a new nation, igniting a fire that will spread across the United States and beyond. The world will feel this heat, this renewal, as we reshape it in our image."

Keeast scanned the faces of his men, each set with grim purpose. He leaned in slightly, his voice low but firm. "Remember, soldiers, we're igniting a revolution. Don't fail!"

Chapter 4

Edge rapped on the door before stepping into Arslan's room. He understood that the longer Arslan remained shut away, the more it would begin to resemble a cell.

"At least, we'll be moving him soon," Edge thought.

The room appeared unchanged from the previous day; the trash still lay untouched, and the stale odor of yesterday's gyros hung heavily in the air.

"Hey there, champ. Just wanted to see how you're holding up," Edge said, sliding a chair beside the bed where Arslan sat, his posture slumped. "Word is you're still tossing and turning at night."

Arslan's eyes were sunken, dark shadows pooling beneath them, giving him the appearance of someone who had spent a sleepless night in a theater of nightmares. He barely lifted his gaze, the weight of fatigue pressing down on him like a heavy shroud. With a slight shake of his head, he communicated his silence, the words trapped behind his lips.

"We located your camera right where you said it would be. It turned out to be a goldmine! We extracted a ton of valuable intel from it," Edge admitted, his voice bright with enthusiasm.

"I've got to give this kid some good news."

Arslan turned his gaze towards Edge, a flicker of anticipation breaking through his otherwise composed demeanor. "Did you uncover who killed my father?" he asked, a faint spark of hope threading through the steadiness of his tone.

"I won't sugarcoat it," Edge said, leaning in slightly, "We haven't pinpointed them yet. But that video? It's a breakthrough. We're zeroing in on whoever is responsible; it's only a matter of time before we close in."

"Can I have my camera back now?"

"Sorry, kid; we still need to extract a lot of information from that camera, so it has to stay locked up in our vault for now. We can't afford to lose anything that might lead us to the men who did this," Edge explained, his tone firm yet sympathetic.

Arslan just looked at Edge, listening to what he was saying and trying to decipher whether Edge was telling him the truth. *"He's been willing to help me, so I guess I can trust him. But honestly, can I really trust anyone right now?"* Arslan thought.

"That's another reason I dropped by, Arslan. Just like the camera, your safety is a priority. We're moving you to a new location—one that's larger, more comfortable, and far safer than this place." Arslan shifted his gaze back to the window, the distant skyline barely registering in his mind. "They've got more to offer than just TV shows," Edge added, injecting a hint of excitement into his voice, hoping to spark some interest. "It should help you get some real rest."

"I just want to go home," Arslan responded dryly.

"I understand. But until I track those responsible down, your safety has to come first. I'll be out of the loop for a few days, and I need to ensure you're secure while I'm away. When I return, I'll share everything I've uncovered about the man who took your father from you."

Arslan offered only a slight nod, his eyes heavy with exhaustion. The remnants of last night's turmoil clung to him like a shroud, but he fought to maintain the composure his father had always demanded. His lips pressed together, a silent vow to embody stoicism even as the weight of grief threatened to crack his facade.

"I'll be back up when they come to move you. If you need anything before then, just ask," Edge instructed.

"Baaraka Allahu fik," Arslan said quietly as Edge stood to leave.

Pausing in his trek to the door, Edge smiled. "'ant kadhalik."

****

Reid, Dana, and Pete hovered near the conference table, their anticipation palpable as they awaited Tucker and Edge to kick off the mission briefing. Reid's mind raced, sifting through the scant details he had been given by Edge.

"Navigate to the heart of a city gripped by martial law to prevent any adversary from seizing an unknown object of questionable significance. That was the most ambiguously clear briefing I'd ever encountered. The kicker? There would be no backup, and this operation was completely off the books. If we got caught by the authorities, it could mean the end of our careers; if the enemy got us, well, that was a death sentence. What's not to love?" Reid finished his internal rant as the mission briefing began.

"Okay, Edge. This is your show," Tucker gestured as he sat down.

The Delta operative loomed at the front of the office, shoulders squared and posture rigid. An air of command radiated from him, a silent declaration that he was in charge. This space, filled with maps and screens, was his territory.

"I'm offering you one final opportunity to back out," Edge said, his voice steady but grave. "Let me be clear: we're defying direct orders. That means no backup, no extraction if things go south. The odds are stacked against us. I can't guarantee that everyone will return."

Edge surveyed the room, noting the reactions of what will be his team. His gaze landed on Crawford, a newcomer who stood just over six feet tall and had the athletic build of a basketball player. Edge hadn't yet had the chance to learn much about him, but his initial impression was of a man eager to dive in. That enthusiasm was commendable, as long as it came with a level-headed approach. Reid had labeled Crawford the "go-to guy," known for his ability to dismantle obstacles to get the job done.

"Ok, then let's get started," Edge pressed the button on the remote, and the monitor flickered to life, revealing a detailed 3-D blueprint of a building, its lines sharp and precise against the dim light of the room.

"Welcome to Global Trust Tower," Edge began, his voice steady as he gestured toward the towering structure on the screen. "Over twenty floors of offices, vaults, steel reinforcements, and concrete walls. Our best guess? The Order is after a financial score. Given the complex web of network security in place, their entry point will likely be the server farm on the eighteenth floor."

With a swift click of the wireless remote, one of the floors in the diagram lit up, rotating to reveal a bird's-eye perspective.

"Given what this group has demonstrated so far, the firewalls and other security features will be nothing more than a speed bump. They are going to get in and get out fast," Edge continued. "They have two likely entry points for the building: the ground floor or the roof. With police and National Guard flooding the streets, a ground approach is far too dangerous. I'm convinced they'll opt for the roof."

Edge shifted his focus to the blueprints of the nineteenth and twentieth floors, his remote in hand. With a steady hand, he activated the laser pointer, illuminating the stairwells that zigzagged through the building's core. "The Order is likely to use these stairwells as their entryway to the server farm," he explained, his voice clear and authoritative. Each flicker of the laser drew attention to the paths they would take, emphasizing the strategic advantage of bypassing the heavily monitored ground level.

"They'll probably deploy a helicopter, disguising it as a rescue operation to breach the no-fly zone, land on the roof, and make a quick exit. This team will possess authentic transponder codes and call signs to pass scrutiny. By the time anyone catches on to their ruse, they'll be long gone. This approach gives them the upper hand. If I were in their shoes, that's exactly how I'd execute it."

Edge returned to the 3-D rendering of the tower, the sleek lines and angles sharp against the dim light. Two sets of vertical columns blinked urgently on the structure.

"Here's our plan to intercept them. The north side of the building features elevators and stairwells that ascend to the rooftop, but they skip several floors along the way. In contrast, the south side holds the only access points to the sixteenth floor and above. This restriction is tied to their security protocols and the presence of restricted zones." Edge clicked the remote again, and the display shifted to reveal the intricate layout of the sixteenth floor.

"To access the floors above sixteen, you'll need to step onto the sixteenth floor first and then navigate through the stairwell located on the right. The network security demands on-site access," Edge explained, his tone serious. "This means we can anticipate a small team stationed on the eighteenth floor. They won't risk any interruptions during their operation. Expect them to establish a heavily fortified perimeter on both the sixteenth and seventeenth floors," using the remote, he started marking locations on the building plan.

"They'll probably erect barricades to block our access to the stairwell. They'll also seal off the corridor leading south to the lawyer's offices, cutting off our only route to the elevators. A hallway like that could easily be held by three men for as long as they need. Even if we somehow managed to push through, the delay would give them ample time to complete their mission and slip away," Edge stated, his gaze sharp and focused as he read each of their faces, to which they all appeared to be waiting for the "but" to follow.

"I'm betting that they're preparing for a head-on assault, not a flanking maneuver," Edge continued, pointing to a large room to the left of the hallway that took up practically the entire west side of the building. "This is the lawyers' library. Spacious, with two entrances leading into the hallway."

Edge tapped the keyboard, and a network of pathways illuminated on the floor plan.

"These are the A/C ducts," he highlighted their position in the library, then pressed the remote; the blueprint faded away, leaving only the ducts visible. A second click adjusted them to their true alignment within the structure. "This duct will take us directly to the library which is accessible from the fifteenth-floor stairwell. There is a catch; right here is a fourteen-foot vertical climb. The only way our plan works is by stealth; if we make too much noise, it's game over. Lucky for us the NSA tactical team has some supplies we can borrow for the night."

Edge pulled a pair of gloves out of his bag and slid them on explaining, "These are the magnetic palm grippers, known as Spider Gear. I'll demonstrate their use in the armory, where we have walls to practice on. With these, we can scale the shaft silently and access the library."

Edge spent the next few minutes detailing their strategy for pushing the enemy back and securing the two floors leading to the server farm. While the element of surprise was crucial, he understood that it alone wouldn't be enough.

"We're facing elite special forces who won't hesitate to eliminate any threats. Stay sharp, everyone. Your instincts will be your greatest asset. The building will be lit by emergency power, so night vision goggles are essential. I trust you three are well-versed in the protocols for entering and clearing a structure?"

"Reid and I have," Crawford spoke up. "We've worked alongside SWAT on breaching teams during raids."

"Has the enemy ever shot at you?" Edge asked.

"A few times, but no sustained firefights," Reid answered. Edge nodded and looked at Dana.

"I've gone through the training and done some raids," she said. "But no shooting was involved."

"Don't let her modesty fool you," Reid said. "She's received a few marksmanship awards."

Edge folded his arms, his brow furrowing as he considered their situation. The odds were shifting against them. He alone had the expertise for a mission of this magnitude. Years of training had taught him to resist the pressure of urgency, yet the gravity of their circumstances compelled him to act now.

These resources were all he had left.

Tucker was an analyst, a role that had kept him firmly rooted in the world of data and strategy, far from the chaos of combat—until yesterday. Now, the weight of responsibility pressed down on him like never before, especially knowing that only three members of his team had ever faced live fire. The urgency for decisive leadership felt more daunting than it ever had, gnawing at him as he contemplated the stakes ahead.

"All right, here's what's going to happen," Edge continued with fervor. "We have to move as a team, and at the right time. You don't move unless I tell you to, or unless your cover is shot to shit, you got that? Move on *my* order only! Coordinated movements may be the only way we will pull this off."

Everyone nodded in understanding.

Tucker walked to the center, next to Edge, "Our main objective is to seize that mainframe, regardless of whether it's occupied. Should this organization successfully access those funds and execute the transfer, they'll gain a virtually endless supply of resources for their next move. The attack on Miami could easily be replicated multiple times. We cannot allow that to happen."

Edge moved to the forefront, ready to wrap up the mission briefing. "Before we head out, I need to say something important. I'm honored to be going into this with all of you. However," he stressed, "if anyone gets hit, do not put yourself in harm's way to save them until the threat has been delt with. We can't afford that kind of risk with our numbers."

Edge allowed his words to hang in the air, watching as the weight of his statement settled over the team. One by one, their heads nodded, the seriousness of the situation etched on their faces. The reality of death loomed large, a specter none of them wanted to confront. Yet, he knew it was a necessary truth to voice, a reminder that they were stepping into a perilous mission where every decision could have fatal consequences.

"Okay, it's time to gear up," Edge concluded.

****

Reid managed to persuade the guards at the armory to take a prolonged coffee break, granting Edge and the team access. As they descended to the large steel cage in the basement, Edge mentally rehearsed the plan: each team member's role, movement strategies, and commands that would cut through the chaos. He brushed aside those thoughts and began selecting weapons from the Department of Homeland Security's arsenal: an array of assault rifles, shotguns, sub-machine guns, and handguns.

Edge selected an MP7A1, its sleek design tailored for close-quarters combat. The foldable iron sights and shortened stock streamlined its profile, while side-mounted rails and a pistol grip enhanced his control. Compact yet deadly, its reliability and precision promised to deliver when it mattered most. He gave a quick glance at the Beretta holstered at his side, a trusted companion that had served him well through countless missions.

"I see that Berretta never leaves your side," Tucker observed.

"Yeah, pretty much married. Every piece in my arsenal is fine-tuned with custom parts—tailored barrels, specialized grips, you name it—ensuring that each round finds its mark. That's why I had no intentions of leaving it at the cabin." He finished with a wink.

Edge passed Tucker a sleek machine gun, its matte finish

glinting under the dim lights. The reflex scope perched atop and the laser sight mounted on the side rail gave it a menacing allure, even if Tucker couldn't recall the specifics of its tactical capabilities. Edge then handed him a standard-issue Glock 9mm, the weight of the weapon settling comfortably in his grip, a laser attachment gleaming ominously beneath the barrel.

He handed Crawford the M4 tactical shotgun, a semi-automatic version that was faster than the typical pump action.

"Yeah, this is going to ruin their day," Crawford said a smile tugging at the corner of his lip as he packed the gun.

The weapons, tactical clothing, vests, and communication equipment went into duffle bags to lower their profile as they left thc building.

"Best to suit up in route. Time was of the essence," Edge said.

Crawford grimaced as he closed the zipper on the heavy bag, feeling its weight pull down on him. "This thing is going to be a beast to carry," he muttered, adjusting his grip to find a more comfortable hold.

"Looks like you can skip leg day for a while," Dana quipped, her fingers deftly sliding flashbangs and smoke grenades into her own tactical bag.

"Listen up, use these only on my command, and when the time comes, keep your head low," Edge said, brandishing a flash-bang with a steely gaze.

"All right," Edge declared, his voice steady as the last weapon was chosen. "Time's ticking, so let's move out. We've got a bank to hit."

Everyone grabbed their bags and filed out of the armory. Crawford lingered at the back, a determined grin spreading across his face. A hefty bag settled on his shoulder as he muttered, "We've got a lot of payback to deliver."

Chapter 5

July 1, 2015
Hours After Bombing
10:30 pm EST

Beneath the heavy shroud of smoke that clung to the Miami skyline, a CH-146 Griffon, cleverly disguised as a medical helicopter, sliced through the murky night. Its course was set for the Global Trust International Bank, a shadowy target amidst the chaos. The air was thick with the whir of rotors as a fleet of genuine medical evacuation helicopters buzzed around, their searchlights sweeping the debris-strewn streets. They transported the injured, their moans mingling with the distant wails of sirens, as they ferried patients from overwhelmed hospitals to makeshift field clinics hastily erected on the outskirts. The Griffon's identification and transponder codes flickered green on the limited air traffic control screens, allowing it to glide through the darkness, undetected and unseen.

The elite Black Unit huddled inside the cramped helicopter, their fingers deftly adjusting night vision goggles and securing gear with practiced precision. In the corner, their leader leaned back, a faint smile playing on his lips as he scrolled through a stream of news updates, absorbing the world's tumultuous response to the attack.

Several members of the team peered out over the city, their faces impassive as they surveyed the chaos below. The devastation unfolded like a grotesque masterpiece, with flames licking at the jagged remnants of buildings and smoke curling into the sky. Heavy machinery churned through the debris, construction crews laboring to restore some semblance of order amidst the wreckage, while emergency vehicles flickered like fireflies, their lights piercing the darkness. "One minute," the pilot announced, his voice steady as he relayed their remaining distance to Keeast.

"Roger that," Keeast nodded, raising a hand to flick the switch on his radio. His squad followed suit, the soft clicks of their devices echoing in the confined space. "We have precisely forty minutes to secure the package once we breach the bank's mainframe. After that, local law enforcement will be alerted. Given the scene out there, I seriously doubt they'll arrive in time for our extraction."

The Griffon touched down with a muted thud on the rooftop helipad, its rotors still whirling as the eight-man squad sprang into action. They spilled out of the helicopter like water from a broken dam, each member instinctively fanning out to cover every angle of the exposed rooftop. Keeast took point, his silhouette cutting through the night as he navigated the gusting winds that swept across the open space. He raised his fist, a silent command that drew his team into formation, their bodies aligning with the door, poised for the next move.

"Lox you're up!" Keeast ordered.

Lox retrieved a silver canister from his supply bag, its surface glinting under the faint rooftop lights. With a firm press of the nozzle, a white, frosty mist erupted, enveloping the door in a chilling haze. He targeted three sections where the internal iron rods lay hidden, the liquid nitrogen hissing as it met the metal. Instantly, the temperature plummeted, the sprayed areas descending to a bone-numbing minus one hundred ninety-six degrees Celsius.

"Strength becomes a weakness," Lox whispered, his fingers deftly positioning three meticulously calibrated explosives on the gleaming white sections of the door. "All set," he announced, stepping back to create a safe distance.

The shaped charge detonated with a thunderous roar, sending a shockwave that rippled through the air. The security rods crumpled like brittle twigs, splintering under the intense pressure. The door, once a solid barrier, swung open with a creaking groan, its hinges protesting as it swayed ominously in the night, revealing the darkened interior beyond.

Keeast signaled Draggo to take point and secure the eighteenth floor. The massive operative guided the team down the tight, spiraling stairs, each step echoing in the confined space. Red emergency lights flickered overhead, but through their night vision goggles, the Black Unit saw only a ghostly green haze. Draggo halted at the door leading to the server farm, his impatience radiating as he glanced back at Hitoshi. The tech expert sprinted up, quickly affixing a sleek hacking device to the access control panel. Draggo, towering and imposing, cast a watchful eye over Hitoshi, the contrast of their sizes stark against the backdrop of the dimly lit corridor.

"I still think you should let Lox blow it," Draggo stated his preference.

Without glancing up from the sleek hacking device, Hitoshi replied, "I've already explained; the network links directly to the security systems. If we blow it, we risk triggering a shut-down command in the mainframe, and we'd lose everything we're after."

"So could that," Draggo grunted as he pointed to Hitoshi's device.

"Only if you make a mistake," Hitoshi schooled him.

The door swung open.

"I don't make mistakes," Hitoshi stated flatly as he detached the device.

Without waiting for Draggo's men to perform a sweep of the room, Hitoshi strode in and made straight for the consoles. "Your job is to provide security. Mine is to defeat their firewalls. Let me worry about my job."

Once the "all clear" signal echoed through their earpieces, Keeast stepped into the room, his gaze flicking to the watch on his wrist.

"*Three minutes ahead of schedule. Perfect,*" Keeast thought as he looked around. "Draggo. Start securing the lower floors," he commanded.

The team swiftly vacated the room, leaving only Keeast and Hitoshi.

The server control area unfolded in a series of tiered consoles, echoing the sleek design of Apollo's mission control. Floor-to-ceiling windows cast a stark divide between the operators and the labyrinth of server cabinets nestled at the heart of the floor. High above, expansive flat-panel displays flickered with vibrant readouts, tracking system statuses, security alerts, and intrusion detection metrics, each glowing like a sentinel over the technological heartbeat of the operation.

Agents of the Order, masquerading as maintenance workers, had infiltrated this space multiple times in the past months, stealthily installing bypasses that provided Hitoshi with a secure entry to the server network. Once he was fully connected, he shot a quick nod to Keeast, signaling that he was ready to proceed.

"Team," Keeast's voice crackled through the radio, sharp and commanding, "we kick off the breach, on my signal. Set your timers for forty minutes. Three... two... one... Mark!"

Fingers danced over the buttons of their watches, each team member synchronizing the timers with a practiced precision.

Hitoshi's fingers danced across the keyboards, a blur of motion reminiscent of a maestro conducting a symphony. Within mere seconds, he crafted the transaction that would siphon funds, the banking networks processing the transfer at lightning speed, ensuring it would be finalized before he even pressed Enter. Most of his focus shifted to manipulating the approval processes, crafting digital illusions to evade any trace-back detection lurking in the shadows.

Hitoshi's fingers flew over the keyboard, crafting an inter-bank transfer that would require a cascade of approvals. Each layer of management loomed like a gauntlet, the Chief Financial Officer himself needing to sign off on the staggering sum displayed on the screen. He had the authentication codes for each executive, a digital keyring ready to unlock the necessary doors. Yet, the real challenge lay in navigating the labyrinthine sign-off system, a web of internal protocols designed to thwart any unauthorized access.

Beyond the typed authentication codes, senior officers relied on biometric readers paired with encrypted verification codes, scrutinized by a distinct security system. This setup introduced delays that could stretch up to an hour, contingent on the transaction size, designed specifically to catch any illicit transfers. Given the magnitude of this transfer, those delays would accumulate to a staggering eight-hour window. Hitoshi faced the daunting task of condensing eight hours of forgery into a mere forty minutes, all while ensuring the system believed the biometric validations were legitimate, that the required intervals were observed, and that this entire operation unfolded under the guise of daylight.

Hitoshi considered the challenge, a slight smirk tugging at one corner of his mouth as he raised a single eyebrow in skepticism.

As Hitoshi launched his digital assault, the rest of the unit was hard at work on the sixteenth floor, transforming the space into a chaotic battleground. Desks toppled over, chairs flew across the room, and filing cabinets clattered to the ground, creating a fortress of debris that would hinder any uninvited guests.

With the area fortified, Lox and Bricks took their positions at the southern end of the main hallway. From that moment on, any intruder stepping onto the floor faced two stark choices: flee or face a hail of bullets.

****

Abandoned cars lay haphazardly across the debris-strewn streets, their rusting frames jutting out like forgotten relics. The chaos of rescue operations allowed Tucker and Reid to slip into the quarantine zone with minimal scrutiny, their demeanor casual yet alert. Edge led the way, a silent sentinel as they navigated the shattered landscape with a mix of urgency and caution. They ducked behind a mound of concrete for fifty feet, barely avoiding the watchful gaze of a National Guard patrol, hearts pounding in sync with the adrenaline coursing through their veins. When the coast was clear, they burst into a sprint, the uneven pavement challenging their footing like an urban obstacle course. Edge moved with practiced agility, weaving through the wreckage effortlessly, while the rest of the team struggled to mirror his fluidity in the dim light.

As they approached the door of Global Trust, Tucker exhaled deeply, a wave of relief washing over him. The team paused, their breaths held, while Edge scanned the area with a hawk-like intensity.

"Looks clear," Edge radioed. "Follow me along the wall. Reid, Crawford, you keep your eyes on the floors above. Tucker, Webster eyes to the right. I've got eyes straight ahead."

The group stepped into the building, shards of glass crunching beneath their boots. The lobby sprawled before them, an expansive space defined by towering pillars and windows that stretched up three stories. Moonlight streamed through, casting a silvery glow over the reception area, where large potted plants stood sentinel beside clusters of plush seating. Despite the remnants of elegance, the atmosphere felt jarring, a dissonance heightened by the chaos lurking just outside. Crawford's mind flickered to Chernobyl, where time had frozen; the scene before him echoed that eerie stillness, as if the space had been vacated mere moments ago.

Edge guided the team toward the north stairwell, his sharp eyes scanning the area for any signs of sentries or patrols. Once he was convinced the area was secure, he took a moment to assess his team, ensuring everyone was alert and ready to move.

"It's quiet," Tucker observed.

"Absolutely, my greatest adversary," Edge shot back, his tone laced with irony. "But from what I can gather, my instincts were spot on. They're waiting above," he said, gesturing toward the ceiling with a steady hand.

"Then why are we crouched in the shadows, speaking in hushed tones?" Tucker questioned, his brow furrowing as he scanned their surroundings.

"Because I only said it 'looks like' my hunch was right," Edge answered. "Okay, enough chit-chat. Night vision only from here," Edge reminded. "Silenced weapons, same order of tasks we said earlier."

Edge turned to Dana, his voice low and steady. "Remember where the cameras are?"

"Top right corner of each stairwell," she responded, her confidence unwavering.

"Perfect," Edge said. "Begin taking out those cameras on the thirteenth floor we work our way to the sixteenth. If they catch a glimpse of us, I want them convinced we're making a direct assault. After we exit the library, be sure to take out the one in the hallway."

Edge understood the enemy's intent to exploit the security network. Their only chance of escaping this precarious situation lay in blinding the ever-watchful surveillance.

"Keep this in mind: if things go sideways and you need to bail, be sure to call for cover fire. The lanes we have to take are vulnerable, and going solo will put you in the crosshairs," Edge warned, disengaging the safety on his weapon with a practiced click. "Alright, let's move."

As they stepped into the stairwell, the oppressive air clung to them like a heavy fog. Reid glanced up for the first time, his eyes widening in disbelief. "Holy shit!" he exclaimed, taking in the daunting number of flights that stretched above them.

Crawford fell into step beside Reid as the others moved ahead. "You remember that hostage situation we got pulled into in

Tampa?" he murmured, his voice barely above a whisper.

"Right, we had to sprint up those ten flights in under ten minutes," Reid reminisced, the memory flooding back with a mix of urgency and nostalgia.

"True, but this is a whole different beast," Crawford chuckled, giving Reid a friendly slap on the shoulder as he passed.

"Appreciate the pep talk," Reid scoffed, keeping his eyes peeled as he continued to safeguarded their six.

Keeping pace with Edge felt like racing against an Olympic sprinter. He darted through the debris-strewn landscape with astonishing speed, his breath steady and controlled, even under the weight of his gear.

"Dear God!" Reid thought, his heart racing. *"Just keep pushing; you're halfway there,"* he urged himself as his legs screamed in protest. Reaching the next stairwell, he caught sight of the sign marking the 4th Floor on the door. "Why did I read that?" he muttered with a sigh.

****

"Sir we have a breach on stairwell E," Hitoshi relayed the information, his gaze fixed on a screen showing live footage from the bank's array of surveillance cameras.

Days prior to the unfolding chaos, the Order deployed a handful of its operatives, masquerading as technicians, to address some so-called 'minor glitches' in the security system. These issues, however, were entirely fabricated. With deft precision, they executed a series of snips and clips, installing wireless transmitters that began relaying all video feeds directly to Hitoshi's computer, ensuring he had eyes on every corner of the operation.

"*Tsk, tsk,*" Keeast responded, watching the small group move up the stairwell. "All right; inform the others. I'd hoped for a quieter night."

"Copy that," Hitoshi acknowledged. "Lox, Bricks, you've got five tangos making their way up stairwell E."

"Confirmed, five tangos," Lox responded. "We'll give them a warm welcome."

"See that you do," Hitoshi replied, his fingers flying over the keyboard as he hacked deeper into the security system.

****

The sharp crack of gunfire rang out in the stairwell as the security camera sputtered and died, sparks flying from its casing. "One more to go," Dana thought, glancing back at Reid as they slipped past Edge and Tucker, who were busy unpacking climbing gear.

"All cameras offline. They're blind," Dana reported.

"Perfect. Head back," Edge answered as he finished equipping his gear. Edge maneuvered to the vent, his fingers deftly loosening the bolts with practiced precision. As he finished, he turned, ready to see his team prepped for action. Instead, he found them still hunched over their gear, struggling with straps and clips. "*This is not your team. Remember that. Gonna take a little more care and feeding to keep them alive.*"

On 9/11, smoke engulfed the upper floors of the World Trade Towers, disorienting and ensnaring victims. In response, Global Trust overhauled their ventilation system to avert a repeat disaster. The new design expelled smoke from each level into the main shaft and out of the building during a fire. Each duct measured three feet by three feet, just wide enough for a person to crawl through, offering the team an ideal access point.

Tucker was the last to close up his bag and before he could say he was ready Edge started, "This is going to be a tight one so be careful and move silently. The duct we need is six feet in. Remember to release your palm from the wall, roll your hand from wrist to fingertips. To release the foot grip just pull your leg away from the wall. It's easy," Edge reminded them before he disappeared into the vent like a mouse into a hole.

The others exchanged glances, apprehension hanging in the air. Dana bounced on her heels, eager to dive in, while Reid and Crawford studied the gloves, practicing the hand motions again. Tucker slipped into the shaft first, followed closely by Reid.

"Don't fall bro," Crawford whispered to Reid before he started his ascent.

"I think I got this."

"Good, because I won't be able to hold up your ass if you don't," Crawford jested.

Reid's fist, his index finger pointing forward, was it being the final part of him to vanish into the narrow opening.

As the walls closed in around them, an unsettling chill crept over Tucker. He couldn't shake the feeling that at any moment, something lurking in the shadows would seize him and drag him into an abyss.

Tucker's gaze fixed on Edge as he twisted onto his back, his body sliding into the vent. In an instant, Edge's feet vanished into the shadowy shaft above. Tucker's heart raced, a knot forming in his stomach as he leaned closer, peering into the inky darkness that loomed ahead.

Rotating onto his back, with the cool metal of the vent against his skin, Tucker hesitated for a moment, then gripped the edges with his gloved hands. He pulled himself upward, inch by inch, the emptiness below him growing more daunting. Following Edge's guidance, he rolled his wrist, feeling the gripper catch onto the surface. With each careful movement, he ascended.

"Hand...leg...hand...leg," Tucker repeated to himself.

Tucker climbed the duct with a measured rhythm, contorting through tight bends as he approached the connection to the sixteenth-floor library. Several times, his hand resisted release, forcing him to perfect the rolling motion before he could move forward.

Tucker finally reached Edge, who perched at the vent's exit, peering down into the room through the slats of the grill.

"What do you see?" Tucker whispered, taking a quiet seat beside him.

Edge raised a finger in a "just a second" signal, his gaze fixed intently on the view beyond the vent.

As the last member of the team slipped into position, Edge leaned in, his voice a low murmur. "Listen up. The op is on track. I'm breaching first to disable the camera in this sector. Once I'm in, you need to move fast. When that feed cuts, they'll be onto us."

The team stripped off their gloves and readied their weapons, tension thick in the air. Edge fingers worked to lose the cover. Tucker held his breath, bracing for the clatter that would echo through the shaft if it slipped from Edge's grip. With a soft thud, the cover landed on the floor, and in a seamless motion, Edge slid through the opening. He swiftly neutralized the camera, each movement precise and practiced, as if he had executed this drill countless times before.

Tucker and the team emerged from the vent into the darkened Lawyer's Library, their eyes adjusting to the muted glow filtering through the far western windows. The rectangular space, a sanctuary for the bank's legal minds, sprawled across the sixteenth floor like a fortress of knowledge. Bookshelves towered against the walls, crammed with leather-bound tomes and case files, while a few massive tables at the center stood empty, their usual occupants displaced. The absence of furniture hinted at recent upheaval; the Order had commandeered the tables to reinforce the hallway, transforming this bastion of legal strategy into a staging ground for their covert operation.

The library's centerpiece, known as the Wall of Tablets, gleamed under the soft lighting. Rows of sleek tablets lined the wall next to the checkout counter, each one a digital repository of the bank's wealth of information. The traditional leather-bound books stood in contrast, their spines worn and familiar, while the tablets offered a modern touch, their screens flickering with data ready to be accessed at a moment's notice.

While it resembled a library at first glance, overflowing with books, sleek computers, and imposing wooden tables, that was where the similarities faded. This space wasn't just any library; it stood as the pinnacle of opulence and sophistication, towering above others in both stature and quality. The collection here outshone even the most prestigious Ivy League libraries, boasting rare volumes and cutting-edge resources that rendered their selections almost pedestrian in comparison.

The library was open to college students twenty-four hours a day, whether they worked at the firm or not, a subtle recruiting technique used to make up for their high turnover rate of entry level positions.

Silence enveloped the library, broken only by the soft, rhythmic breaths of Edge and his team. With the district plunged into darkness, the room lay shrouded in an impenetrable blackness, each shadow deepening the sense of foreboding that hung in the air.

Chapter 6

"Any idea where they are?" Lox radioed, aware that an unsettling amount of time had passed since he was alerted to the presence of intruders, yet the hallway remained eerily still.

Hitoshi let out an exasperated breath, his fingers dancing over the keys of his laptop as he scrolled through the camera feeds. "All stairwell cameras are down; tangos not in sight."

"Why the hell would they be hanging out in the stairwell?" Bricks asked over the comms.

Hitoshi changed his camera screen to show all the cameras around Lox and Bricks. "*Bastards have no concept of patience,*" he thought. Then something caught his eye; another camera went offline, but this one was not in the stairwell. "*Lox and Brinks are being flanked,*" Hitoshi took the realization as another inconvenience, the way someone reacts to their shoe being untied. "Lox, the tangos somehow got into the library. Probably through the A/C ducts."

"Library, check. En route," Lox responded.

"Finally," Bricks mumbled, eager for action.

Lox and Bricks glided across the floor, bodies low and tense. Just a few feet from the library's entrance, they pressed against the cool wood of the checkout counters, their breaths shallow and measured. Every sound felt amplified in the stillness as they edged forward, eyes scanning for any sign of movement.

Bricks caught sight of the silhouettes gliding stealthily across the polished floor near the tables. He raised his hand, fingers forming silent signals. "Five tangos," he communicated, his eyes narrowing as he focused on the threat.

"I'll drop the left, you take the right," Lox signaled with swift hand signs of his own. "On my mark."

A helicopter roared past the window, its piercing searchlight slicing through the darkness like a knife, flooding the room with a fleeting, false dawn.

In the fleeting glow, Edge caught sight of two figures huddled in the corner by the Wall of Tablets. The glimmer revealed the unmistakable outline of a firearm, its cold metal glinting ominously.

"Everyone down... NOW!" he yelled, diving for cover.

Realizing the surprise was gone, Bricks and Lox sprang to their feet, unleashing a hail of gunfire. Bullets zipped past Edge's team, shattering the windows with explosive force. A gust of wind rushed into the library, sending loose papers swirling like leaves caught in a storm.

"Flip the tables!" Edge yelled as bullets ricocheted around them.

With adrenaline surging, Dana hurled a table aside, the heavy wood crashing to the floor as she dove behind it for cover. She squeezed the trigger of her silenced MP7, the weapon barking softly as it spat bullets into the checkout counter, sending splinters flying in a flurry of chaos.

Crawford, Tucker, Reid, and Edge followed suit, forcing the two soldiers to cover. Seizing the opportunity, Edge pushed the offensive. "Tucker, Reid, flank right. Crawford, Dana, fan left."

The team burst from their cover, darting through the library's maze. Tables flew aside with a crash, splintering under the force of their urgency. They maneuvered between towering shelves, shadows weaving amidst the chaos as they sought strategic angles. Each footfall echoed against polished floors.

Lox's eyes zeroed in on the tallest figure, their movements predatory as they prowled the library. He squeezed the trigger, but his bullets trailed just behind the target, missing by inches. In that split second, Tucker hit the ground, instinctively seeking the floor's cold embrace as chaos erupted around him.

Edge's gaze darted over the table, locking onto Lox as rifle flashes painted his black armor in bursts of light. "Enough of this," Edge thought, squeezing the trigger. A controlled burst ripped through the air, aimed at Lox's head. In a split second, Lox dropped, the bullets whizzing past so closely that he felt the rush of air against his helmet. Instinctively, Reid and Tucker retaliated, firing high above the counter. Tablets flew from their mounts, crashing down like shattered dreams, raining debris onto Lox as chaos erupted around them.

The battle morphed into a frantic back-and-forth, each side darting out to unleash a barrage of bullets. Shelves shuddered as paper and books detonated from their perches, caught in the gusts of chaos that swept through the library, swirling like snowflakes in a storm.

Dana had anticipated a day like this, but the reality of a full-blown firefight was far beyond her imagination. She slammed another magazine into her weapon, the metallic click echoing in her ears, and focused on her sights. Each heartbeat pounded in her chest, threatening to drown out the chaos around her.

Crawford thrived in the chaos, relishing the clash against the Order. To him, they were just thugs, ripe for elimination. As a tablet crashed down on one of the soldiers, a flicker of opportunity ignited within him. He switched to his shotgun, sprinting to the counters with purpose. In one fluid motion, he vaulted over the edge, weapon raised, aiming squarely at the soldier's head. But the shotgun kicked back hard, jolting him off target.

"*SHIT!*" Crawford swore as the shot sailed above his target's head. He fired again and again, each pull of the trigger met with a hollow click as his magazine emptied. Dust swirled in the aftermath, revealing his missed opportunity. Dropping to his knees, he ducked as bullets whizzed overhead. Heart racing, he fumbled to reload, slamming shells into the chamber. This time, he vowed, he wouldn't miss.

Edge saw Crawford's run. "Pete hold!" he yelled after him.

The man either ignored him or was too caught up in the moment to acknowledge him. Edge had to give the man credit because his ambush worked... up until he missed with every shot. "*He's letting adrenaline take over,*" Edge diagnosed.

"Reid! Tucker! Go full auto on them now!" Edge ordered.

At Edge's command, Tucker and Reid flipped their weapons to full auto, fingers dancing over the triggers. A storm of bullets erupted, shredding the counter into splinters. As dust and debris hung in the air, the two enemy soldiers stumbled back, firing wildly as they fled the library, desperate to escape the onslaught.

Like a predator catching the scent of blood, Crawford sprang to his feet, eyes locked on the retreating figures slipping through the door. He surged forward, muscles coiling, hot on their heels.

"*Ah, fuck,*"*Edge propelled himself over the barricade, adrenaline surging as he sprinted after the retreating figures.*

Crawford swore as the soldiers slipped through another door, vanishing from sight. He sprinted forward, weapon braced against his shoulder, adrenaline surging through his veins. As he neared the doorway, his gaze darted across the hallway, catching glimpses of the lawyers' offices beyond.

Two imposing cubicles loomed five feet ahead, their stark lines contrasting with the chaotic backdrop. A flicker of movement caught his attention—something that disrupted the rigid geometry of the space. Just as he prepared to advance, a powerful grip seized him, yanking him off to cover as if he were nothing more than a sack of potatoes.

"What the fuck?" he began to shout when a hail of bullets ripped through the air, striking the spot where he had just stood. A strong hand clamped down on his chin, forcing his gaze to meet the furious eyes of Edge.

"I said *no* hero bullshit! You don't move unless *I* say! You got it!?" Edge repeated with enough force that Crawford felt it in his soul.

"Gotcha," Crawford nodded sharply, his eyes wide with understanding.

"You want to follow them, use this to clear the way," Edge yanked Crawford's flashbang from his vest. Crawford glanced at the device and then back at Edge, uncertainty flickering in his eyes as if weighing the implications of accepting it. He hesitated, but when Edge shook the flashbang in front of him with urgency, Crawford snatched it from his hand.

"Reid, Tucker, stack up across from us. Webster, over here with me," Edge spoke once his anger subsided. As they shifted into their designated spots, Edge leaned into the doorway, peering into the law offices. His sharp eyes scanned the room, quickly identifying the soldiers lurking within. *"I got you now."*

"Reid, send your flashbang rolling across the hall. Crawford, wait for the cue and launch yours high—aim for above the cubicles," Edge ordered, his voice low but firm.

Reid sent the small grenade skittering across the polished floor. It tumbled into the law offices, where it erupted in a blinding flash, bathing the room in white light. The deafening roar of one hundred seventy decibels shattered the tense silence, a sonic wave that disoriented anyone caught without proper gear.

Crawford's grenade arced high, soaring past Reid's before detonating in a brilliant flash overhead. Edge sprinted to the doorway, eyes scanning for any sign of movement. The silence felt heavy, pressing against him. Satisfied, he shot a quick signal to the team—time to move.

"Eyes up: they're waiting for us," he warned.

Edge led the charge into the lawyers' offices, his eyes darting for any flicker of movement. Crawford and Dana split left, their bodies low, weapons raised, while Reid and Tucker veered right, each step deliberate and calculated. The air crackled with tension as they advanced.

The office sprawled larger than anticipated, accommodating two rows of sizable cubicles and glass-walled offices lining the edges. The narrow walkways between the cubicles could fit two people side by side, but offered limited routes for maneuvering.

"There aren't many places for them to hide. So where are they?" Edge wondered.

He had anticipated the flashbangs would create an opening for his team. It was a tactic he'd employed successfully in similar situations: throw one in to flush out the unsuspecting, then follow up with another for those clever—or fortunate— enough to evade the first.

The plan had succeeded, though not flawlessly. Lox and

Bricks ducked from the first flashbang, timing their emergence just as the second one exploded. Most would have been disoriented, but Keeast's team was anything but average. They dropped behind cover, evading the blast with practiced precision.

The flashbang's blinding light forced them to ditch their night vision, leaving them in a murky silence, shadows flickering in the dim office. Edge's team moved with caution, but the soft thuds of bodies colliding with furniture betrayed their position.

Bricks strained to listen, gauging their proximity by the muffled sounds around him. After a resounding crash echoed nearby, he grinned, pinpointing the perfect target for his next shots.

****

Amid the chaos unfolding below, Keeast perched in the most luxurious chair he could find—a sleek, ergonomically designed desk seat most likely cost a pretty penny. He leaned back, his fingers steepled as he observed Hitoshi deftly infiltrate the bank's digital fortress, the glow of the screens illuminating their determined faces. The distant sounds of gunfire and shouts created a stark contrast to the calmness of his temporary refuge, where comfort enveloped him like a cocoon.

"*Not bad,*" he thought as he settled down on the fabric, propping one foot across his knee. "How much longer till the transfer is complete?"

Hitoshi sat before three twelve-inch LCD screens, seemingly oblivious to the chaos unfolding below. As he neared the end of his assignment, timing became critical. His programs had handled much of the work earlier; now, the responsibility lay squarely on him.

Hitoshi kept typing on the portable keyboard. A single beep indicated that he had completed another step. The tapping of the keyboard paused. "Ten minutes until completion," Hitoshi responded confidently.

"Lox, Bricks? What's the situation? Over," Keeast radioed.

Three static blips came over the radio, the signal his team used when answering would give away their position.

"Draggo, eyes up," Keeast transmitted. "Lox and Bricks are engaged in the library, but be advised—hostiles could be heading your direction shortly."

A deep, guttural voice with a heavy Russian accent crackled through the radio. "Do you have eyes on them?" Draggo inquired, referring to Lox and Bricks.

"That's a negative; the intruders shot out the cameras. They're alive, just not able to communicate," Keeast answered.

"How much time until we're done?" Draggo asked.

"Approximately eight minutes."

"Copy that. I'm bringing Lox and Bricks in; we'll hold the line here," Draggo transmitted.

✳✳✳✳

Dana crouched low, her eyes scanning the office aisle for any flicker of movement. With a quick nod, she gestured for Crawford to advance to the next cubicle. Edge had laid out the plan: they would leapfrog, each pair moving with precision while staying low, avoiding the exposed tops of the cubicles. One covered while the other slipped forward. Reid and Tucker mirrored their movements on the right, shadows weaving through the chaos. Edge remained a few feet back, his gaze sweeping the cubicle tops, ready to provide backup and keep the enemy pinned down.

The team advanced with caution, but the cluttered desks betrayed them; every small object seemed to rattle like a child's toy at even the faintest touch. Crawford gestured sharply, indicating it was Dana's turn to slip forward.

"Why haven't they attacked yet? Are they even here?" She wondered as she reached her next position. A flicker of movement caught Dana's eye. She shot up a clenched fist, her heart racing as she signaled Crawford to halt. But his eagerness clouded his judgment; he misread her gesture as a cue to advance. As he darted forward, Dana's eyes widened in alarm. She shook her fist again, urgency surging through her, but it was too late. Crawford was already committed, veering into the nearest cubicle.

Crawford's sudden shift sent him crashing into the file cabinets suspended beneath the desk. The jolt reverberated through the furniture, sending a baseball teetering on the edge of the shelf before it tumbled to the floor with a dull thud.

The world seemed to halt. Crawford's gaze locked onto Webster, his eyes bulging as the object rolled and ricocheted across the floor. Despite the night vision goggles shielding his eyes, Dana could almost hear the frantic thoughts racing through his mind. *"Son a bitch!"*

They took a moment to exhale, the tension hanging thick in the air. The room remained frozen, a silent tableau awaiting the next move.

The cubicle's fabric wall erupted, bullets tearing through the air as Crawford hit the ground, flattening himself against the cold floor. Dana caught a glimpse of the muzzle flash from a nearby cluster of cubicles. She fired back, but instead of silencing the enemy, she drew their fire, rounds slamming into her position. Papers and office supplies cascaded from the walls, showering her in a chaotic downpour.

Gunfire erupted from Edge, Tucker, and Reid, but their shots found only air.

Crawford rolled onto his back, spotting a gaping hole in the wall. The enemy's attention was locked on Dana, giving him a fleeting moment of opportunity. He squeezed the trigger, unleashing a rapid stream of bullets through the opening. Each shot echoed in the chaos, but he couldn't tell if he struck anything. At least the enemy fire had ceased, leaving a tense silence in its wake.

"You alright?" Crawford yelled with a whisper into his radio.

"Never better," she replied sarcastically. "Edge, what do you see?"

"Two hostiles spotted," Edge reported, his voice steady. "Approximately thirty feet from your location. Reid and Crawford, provide cover fire. Dana and Tucker, flank them from either side. Then switch positions. I'll keep them pinned down. On my mark: GO!"

Crawford and Reid unleashed a barrage of bullets toward the enemy's position. Edge kept his eyes peeled, scanning for movement. Suddenly, a gun barrel breached the cubicle wall to his right. Without hesitation, he squeezed off three rapid shots; the weapon clattered down, vanishing from view. With adrenaline rushing through him, Edge pushed forward.

"Come on, show yourself," Edge mentally coaxed them. A right arm emerged, brandishing a handgun, blind firing they unleashed a hail of bullets down the center aisle. Edge instinctively dove into a nearby cubicle as the rounds zipped past him. He quickly peeked out, catching sight of one soldier sprinting down

the aisle while another provided cover fire during the retreat.

"Motherfucker!" Edge exclaimed as he rolled back. "They're retreating down the middle. They've got me suppressed."

"Tucker, keep an eye on the aisle," Reid instructed as he stood up to fire on the retreating soldiers. "Edge, you're clear."

"Reid! Hit the deck!" Tucker shouted as a soldier's gunfire erupted over the wall.

Reid dropped instantly as rounds sailed overhead.

"You good?" Tucker asked.

"That was way too close!" Reid panted. "Appreciate it."

The battle shifted abruptly. Both sides bobbed up and down like players in a whack-a-mole game. Edge noted the enemy's discipline; their corner coverage and rapid weapon cycling allowed them to fend off his five-man team effectively. Yet, they were still retreating.

Crawford noticed the duo nearing the bend at the end of the office corridor. If he reached that position first, he could block their escape.

"Webster! Cover me!" he yelled. Before she could respond he was moving down the aisle, shotgun out. He fired every time the enemy tried to poke their head out. *"Yeah, now I've got you!"*

The nearest enemy rose into view, but before Crawford could steady his aim, the man ducked out of sight. In a heartbeat, his partner emerged, gun raised. Two sharp cracks echoed through the chaos. Crawford never registered the shots; one struck him in the neck, the other entered his temple. He crumpled against the wall, leaving a crimson streak in his wake.

Dana's heart raced as she stared in disbelief at Crawford's lifeless body sprawled on the floor. Bullets whizzed past her, slicing through the air. She cautiously lifted her head above her cover, spotting two figures sprinting around the corner, urgency fueling their escape.

"Crawford's down! I repeat Crawford's down! They're falling back around the corner," she cried out desperately.

Reid felt like he'd just been slapped. "Crawford's been shot? Is he ok?"

Dana shook her head, even though no one would see. "No...he is not."

"Hold it together people. Reid, Tucker, follow me. Dana, check on Crawford," Edge voice came over the radio.

Reid slammed his fist against the wall, frustration boiling beneath the surface, yet he kept his cool. He and Tucker trailed Edge as they rounded the corner, spotting the two men darting through the door and into the hallway.

Reid approached Dana, who knelt beside Crawford. Blood pooled around his head, a crimson river trickling down to his neck. The wound was fatal, and the reality of their loss hung heavy in the air.

"Goddamit, man," Reid mumbled.

Dana pulled the few spare magazines that remained on Crawford's vest.

"We're going to need these," she said, dejectedly. Reid nodded silently, his expression hardening as he turned away, striding purposefully toward Edge.

"They're going upstairs," Reid said, looking at Edge. "Do we go after them?"

"Negative. There's more than two of them up there, and I'll bet my shitty salary they're waiting for us," Edge answered.

"Then they'll slaughter us," Tucker concluded more to himself than anyone in particular.

"We can't just let them get away. Is there another way up?" Reid stated with a sense of certainty.

"We need the code to get to next floor by the other stairs," Tucker stated.

Edge flicked up his night vision goggles, the green hue illuminating his focused expression as he turned to Tucker. "You just hit the jackpot," he said, a glint of mischief in his eyes. Without hesitation, he lunged for the scattered papers on the desk, shoving them into a nearby garbage bucket with swift, deliberate motions.

Tucker assisted Edge in stacking three overflowing piles of paper atop a battered desk, confusion swirling in his mind about how this peculiar task had suddenly become Edge's new mission. The papers fluttered slightly in the draft, remnants of frantic moments now reduced to clutter.

"Three things to always have on a mission, no matter where you are: money, smokes, and a lighter," Edge said as he struck the metal wheel on his Zippo and was rewarded with a steady, solid flame.

Tucker looked at him, puzzled, as he set the pale on fire. "Umm, how is this helping us?"

"Those locked doors can only be opened with a code," Edge began. "But if there's a fire, the alarm triggers automatic overrides, unlocking all exits to ensure everyone can escape. It's part of the fire safety regulations."

Tucker had to chuckle, "I would've never thought of that."

"Okay, everyone. We're gonna get wet in a second. Now grab your stuff and follow me."

Edge sprinted ahead, with Tucker and Dana close behind. A blaring alarm shattered the tension, and the sprinklers erupted, drenching the floor in a cascading deluge. Reid lingered for a heartbeat, his gaze locked on Crawford's lifeless form. Gritting his teeth, he slammed a fresh magazine into his weapon and charged after his team.

✳✳✳✳

"Draggo?" Keeast asked said over the radio.

"Sir?"

"Have you handled the intruders yet?" he asked, his fingers twirling his handgun on the desk.

"Negative on the stairs, sir. Lox reported they were tailing him and Bricks," Draggo said, his tone clipped. "We've been in position for about a minute, over."

Keeast exhaled sharply, frustration etched across his features. The incessant wail of the fire alarms grated on his nerves, making it nearly impossible to concentrate. "Hitoshi, can't you silence those damn alarms?"

The computer whiz paused his furious typing, swiveling his chair to confront a different keyboard. With three exaggerated keystrokes, he shot a glare that clearly conveyed "don't interrupt me," and just like that, the cacophony ceased. He turned back to his original task, resuming his work without uttering a single word.

Keeast never offered apologies; as the head of the unit, he believed he had earned that right. Few dared to confront him about interruptions, their fear keeping them silent. Yet, when Hitoshi immersed himself in his work, even Death would think twice before disturbing him.

Silence replaced the blaring alarms, yet the lights continued to strobe, casting an erratic glow across the room. Keeast's gaze flicked to a sign above one of the doors, its "Emergency Exit" illuminated in stark white, an arrow directing the way out. A smirk crept onto Keeast's lips as he pieced together the

67

intruders' scheme.

"Looks like someone's been doing their homework," Keeast said, a wry smile creeping onto his face. "Draggo, get your team to the northwest stairwell, now. We've got tangos heading for the secondary barricade. They're using the fire alarms to slip past the door locks. Move it!"

"Moving out now," Draggo confirmed.

"Your mission is to contain the targets. Eliminate if necessary, but prioritize your safety. We're under five minutes to go," Keeast directed, his tone clipped and authoritative. "Just hold them off until we're done."

No response came from the Russian. The head of Black Unit took a second to contemplate the success this team was having. *"Perhaps I have underestimated them? Could these few intruders get the best of my men?"* Keeast asked himself. A thunderstorm of his team's weapons erupted directly beneath them. "Not likely," he said with satisfaction.

Chapter 7

The seventeenth-floor reception area exuded opulence, designed to captivate the bank's elite clientele. At its heart, a plush waiting room beckoned, surrounded by sleek research offices that hugged the west and east walls. A narrow hallway, flanked by rich wood-paneled half-walls and elegant etched glass partitions, connected these spaces, leading to a grand marble staircase that spiraled upward towards the CEO's office. Every detail, from the polished surfaces to the ambient lighting, was meticulously curated to shape the client's impression of the bank.

Whenever the elevator doors slid open it revealed the reception desk, where visitors signed in. From there they would be guided into the waiting room, a sanctuary of lavish chairs and inviting couches. Refreshments glimmered on a polished side table, while large tropical plants flourished in every corner, their vibrant greens contrasting with the rich hardwood floors. This space, with its luxurious touches, transformed the mundane wait for an appointment into a brief escape from the day.

While clients settled into their seats, they could discreetly watch the activities unfolding in the Research Offices just across the hall. The Research Offices, a source of pride for the bank, resembled a high-tech library. Equipped with cutting-edge computers and video screens, the space continuously monitored global events, broadcasting a clear message to clients: *We are aware of everything, to safeguard your investments.*

In its abandoned state, the once-luxurious atmosphere felt cold and uninviting, a stark departure from its original intent.

Draggo and his squad moved cautiously toward the makeshift barricade at the west end of the waiting area, their eyes scanning for threats. A thick gray fog surged into the reception, swallowing the opulent surroundings and triggering a cacophony of fire alarms. Recognizing the smoke grenade's telltale plume, Draggo signaled his team to halt, weapons ready, as they melded into the shadows cast by the swirling haze. The barricade, once a mere precaution, now lay concealed within the eerie shroud.

"Clever Fuckers. They got to the barricade before us," Draggo cursed to himself.

"Watch out for flash-bangs," Draggo instructed as his finger rested gently on his weapons trigger. With the room stripped of furniture and the barricades rendered useless, Draggo and his team stood vulnerable.

The blaring fire alarms fell silent, leaving an unsettling stillness in the air. The strobe of emergency lights flickered, casting erratic shadows across the floor. Soldiers of the Order pushed their night-vision goggles up to their foreheads, eyes adjusting to the harsh glow as they peered into the haze.

The Order recognized that the intruders had a penchant for deploying flash-bangs, and the blinding bursts rendered through night-vision goggles were particularly dangerous. Even a brief moment of blindness could prove fatal, leaving a soldier unable to react or defend against an imminent threat.

Black Unit remained tense, muscles coiled like springs, eyes locked on the swirling smoke. Whispers of doubt flickered among them—had they been lured into a trap? Just as uncertainty began to settle, two shadowy figures erupted from the fog, sprinting toward the Research Offices, their movements swift and purposeful.

"Tango sighted," shouted one of Draggo's team members piercing the tension, and triggered a chorus of gunfire from the entire unit.

****

Shards of glass rained down around Edge and Reid as they hit the floor, instinctively tucking their bodies low. "Stay low, keep your head down," Edge urged, his voice a low growl.

"I hadn't thought of that," Reid replied sarcastically as he swept a shot up picture frame out of his path.

Gunfire erupted like a relentless storm, compelling them to dart forward as shards of glass, scattered books, and splintered furniture erupted around them. The partition crumbled under the barrage, bullets puncturing the exterior windows with deafening cracks. A gust of wind rushed in, swirling debris into the air like a blizzard, cloaking Edge and Reid in chaotic cover as they pressed on.

Edge's strategy involved advancing through the Research section from the west, then shifting south to flank the enemy from the east. Based on how the bullets tore through the air, he indicated that the Order had settled somewhere in the center of the floor.

"At least the plan is working so far," Edge thought as they made their move.

As the Order's attention wavered, Tucker and Dana bolted from the thinning smoke, their boots pounding against the floor as they raced toward the barricade. Without hesitation, they unleashed a barrage of gunfire, the sharp cracks echoing through the chaos. Outnumbered yet resolute, they seized the advantage, transforming the precarious situation into a tactical opportunity.

Under fire, the Order scrambled to adapt, facing threats from two fronts. "Split up!" Draggo barked, his voice cutting through the chaos. "Half of you, hold the barricade! The rest, keep those two in the Research Offices pinned down!"

"Got it, Draggo!" a soldier shouted, adjusting his grip on his weapon as he moved into position.

"Don't let them breathe!" Draggo urged, eyes darting between the smoke and the targets.

The team sprang into action, instinctively falling into formation, each member focused on their objective. The air erupted with gunfire, bullets zipping in every direction.

Draggo crouched low, his gaze locked on the chaos unfolding. He tracked the movements of the two figures darting through the Research Offices, their path leading them closer to a vulnerable angle that would soon lay his men bare.

"They're trying to flank us," Draggo muttered.

The waiting room offered no refuge for combat, its design working against the soldiers' advantage.

Draggo's eyes locked onto a sizable gap in the research office partitions—the only path the two men would have to cross, creating a window of opportunity for him to strike. He slipped behind a massive planter, its lush leaves cascading like a verdant curtain, blending into the shadows. He focused on his breathing, steadying his aim as he prepared to unleash his shot.

****

"Tucker how you are you guys holding up over there?" Edge radioed.

"Getting shot at. Otherwise, we're great," Tucker replied sharply.

"Okay. Keep it up; we're nearly there," Edge continued with labored breathes.

Edge noticed the gap between the two walls, making rolling or jumping pass impossible; they had no choice but to sprint across the exposed ground. He looked at Reid and instructed, "It's a few feet, but it leaves us completely exposed, so we need to hustle."

Reid nodded in understanding as he slung his gun across his back. "One...two...Go!" Edge signaled, and the two men took off together.

Concealed in the darkness, Draggo meticulously aligned his aim, focusing on the second of the two figures. A smirk crossed his lips as he pulled the trigger, striking his target with unerring accuracy.

Edge pressed his back against the wall, heart racing as he glanced over at Reid. Just a few steps from safety, Reid's body lurched to the right, propelled by an unseen force. He stumbled forward, collapsing in a tangled heap at the entrance. Without hesitation, Edge lunged forward, grasping Reid's arm and yanking him to cover. The moment registered—Reid's hand clutched a gaping wound in his neck, crimson seeping through his fingers, painting the ground beneath them.

"Reid, stay with me!" Edge shouted, desperation clawing at

his throat as he locked eyes with his teammate. Blood oozed from between fingers, like a dark promise. Disappointment surged within Edge; he felt helpless as Reid's grip slackened, his head lolling to the side, life slipping away like sand through fingers.

"Goddamn it!" He barked through gritted teeth, as he laid Reid's body down.

Edge forced himself to focus, knowing there would be time for the others to grieve later. He quickly scavenged ammunition from Reid's vest, feeling the weight of loss settle heavily on his shoulders. With two teammates down, he realized they could no longer push forward; regrouping and retreating were now their only viable options.

"One tango neutralized in the southern offices. All units, advance and engage remaining hostiles," Draggo commanded.

"Copy that squad leader, moving in," a soldier's voice responded.

"Awe Hell!" Edge exclaimed as several soldiers closed in on his position. He quickly radioed Tucker, "Reid's down! We need to pull back!"

"What the fuck?" Tucker responded. "Are you sure? What happened?"

"No time. Just throw that last flash-bang into the center of them now!" Edge continued.

Tucker gripped the flash-bang tightly, his heart pounding in sync with the chaos around him. With a swift motion, he hurled the grenade into the heart of the waiting room. It sailed through the air, a heartbeat later, a blinding light erupted, flooding the space with searing brightness and an ear-splitting bang that momentarily swallowed the sound of gunfire.

Savoring his success, Draggo shifted his focus to the last two opponents holed up nearby. With their defenses crumbling, it was time to eliminate the remaining threats. As he turned, a glint caught his eye—a metallic canister hurtling toward his men.

"Flash-bang!" Draggo yelled just as the grenade detonated just above the floor's surface.

A few of his soldiers managed to dodge the blast, but Draggo and several others were not as fortunate, left dazed and momentarily immobilized.

The bang was all Edge needed. He quickly hopped over the half wall and sprinted through the research area, his boots crushing everything from papers to keyboards.

"Time's running short, go faster, go faster," he encouraged himself as he hurdled a broken chair.

Peeking over the barricade Tucker spotted Edge in a full-tilt sprint. "What...in...the...world is he thinking?"

"I'm not sure but let's make sure he makes it," Dana said, as the two provided suppressing fire.

The flash-bang had hit a few of the Black Unit, but many had been protected enough that the effects wore off quickly. Draggo, as a matter of sheer will, shrugged off the disorientation and went hunting for Edge.

"Time to end all this bullshit, for good," Draggo muttered through gritted teeth, his thumb slide along the surface of his weapon, to flick one the laser sight which glided menacingly toward his target.

Dana's gaze locked onto a crimson laser cutting through the smoky haze, originating from behind a towering plant. The leaves rustled, hinting at movement within. In an instant, she pivoted her weapon toward the shadow, unleashing a storm of bullets that shattered the vase and sent shards of glass flying.

The colossal plant toppled, dragging Draggo down into the chaos, obscuring him from view.

Edge navigated the maze of walls and pillars, each step a careful dance with danger. But as he rounded the corner, an expanse of open space loomed ahead, stark and unforgiving. He could almost feel the weight of the enemy's gaze, locked onto him like a predator stalking its prey. He knew—once he broke into the open, there would be no refuge. Death awaited him in that exposed stretch, a certainty he couldn't shake.

"Unless... Nah'; too risky. But then again what choice do I have?"

Edge sprang onto a nearby desk, launching himself into the air. The enemy scrambled to recalibrate, their focus shifting as they pursued him instead of anticipating his next move. He hit the ground in a roll, seamlessly sliding behind a sturdy barricade. Heart pounding, he scanned his body for any signs of injury, then met Dana's gaze, their silent connection a brief moment of reassurance amidst one hell of a night.

"Are you insane," she said, and fired off a controlled burst.

"What the hell just happened?" Tucker demanded, glancing at Edge as he ducked into cover beside him, bullets whizzing overhead. "What about Reid?""

He shook his head. "We need to retreat," Edge gasped, breathless. "We've lost our advantage. The Order is in control now!"

"Tucker shook his head, urgency lacing his voice. "No, Edge, we can't retreat now. We've given up too much to turn back."

"Tucker, we have no other option. Our only chance is to survive and fight another day. If we go down, they win; we can't honor the dead if we're lying beside them," Edge insisted.

"Forget it; they're falling back," Dana interjected.

As silence took hold once more, Tucker and Edge took a

moment to peer around their cover just in time to see the Order in full retreat. The atmosphere became eerily quiet, punctuated only by the rhythmic thud of boots striking the floor as Tucker and Edge peered carefully from their cover. Their eyes widened at the sight of the Order, falling back, shadows darting away like phantoms of the night.

✳✳✳✳

As Draggo pushed himself off the floor, his communicator crackled to life with Keeast's voice. "Team leader, the package has been transferred. Get your squad to the extraction point."

"What about the intruders, sir?" Draggo growled, frustration boiling within him.

"They are not the focus of this mission. We'll deal with them later," Keeast explained.

"No...we can finish them now," Draggo spat, as blood trickled down his face. He winced as he dug into his skin, feeling the sharp sting of glass embedded beneath the surface. With a swift tug, he extracted the jagged shard, its edge glinting ominously—a remnant of the shattered vase that had exploded.

Draggo's radio crackled to silence, and then Keeast's voice cut through the static with a steady, authoritative tone that brooked no argument. "Soldier you have your orders. Fall back now!"

Draggo bristled at the thought of following orders, but he understood that Keeast had zero tolerance for insubordination—one of the rare few he respected enough to heed. For a tense moment, he examined his weapon, blood trickling down to obscure his vision.

"Black Unit, fall back," he finally barked.

The team fell back with military precision, weapons trained on potential threats, ensuring every angle was covered as they ascended the stairs.

Dana entered into the waiting area with weapon raise. The tall figure sprinted up the stairs, after casting her an intense glare. "Who was that guy?" she exclaimed, bewilderment flooding her voice. "I thought he was finished for good!"

"I'm not sure," Edge replied, as he came to her side.

"We've got to get them before they leave," Tucker shook his head, determination etched on his face. He stepped forward, intent on reaching the stairs.

"Hold it. We don't know if they're leaving. There could be another trap up there—"

Before Edge could complete his thought, Tucker bolted toward the stairs, urgency propelling him forward. In a flash, Edge surged after him, his legs pumping furiously. He closed the gap in an instant, seizing Tucker's tactical vest with a firm grip, yanking him back just as they neared the stairwell.

"You wanna die too?" Edge yelled . "That's how you plan to stop them?" Edge's gaze locked onto Tucker's, a fierce urgency coursing between them. Just then, a crimson light pulsed ominously from a black box nestled in the shadows of the stairwell.

"DOWN!" Edge yelled, yanking Tucker backward as the remote device erupted, hurling shards of marble, splintered concrete, and twisted metal into the air.

As the dust hung in the air, Tucker and Edge pushed themselves upright, their eyes fixed on the crumbling stairs. Frustration etched deep lines on their faces, a silent acknowledgment of the Order's escape and the mission's dismal outcome. Tucker's fists clenched, a familiar rage simmering beneath the surface.

He drew his pistol, each step toward the stairs fueled by a surge of fury, and squeezed the trigger, unleashing a barrage of bullets into the empty void above.

He squeezed the trigger repeatedly, the empty gun clicking in protest, the slide locked back and mocking him with its silence. Gradually, his arms fell to his sides, the adrenaline draining away, leaving only a heavy weight of despair where fury once burned. "What did we do wrong? We had them!" Tucker barked in frustration.

"We didn't do anything wrong. This is war," Edge answered calmly.

"I don't mean to be a burden but—"

They spun around to see Dana collapsed on the floor, her right pant leg soaked in crimson. A jagged shard of metal protruded from her thigh, the remnants of the explosion that had rocked the room.

Edge and Tucker raced to her side. Edge tore his sleeve free, fabric ripping with a sharp sound, and pressed it against her bleeding thigh, applying firm pressure to staunch the flow of blood.

"What next?" she grunted.

Before either could speak, red lights flickered to life, bathing the room in a sinister glow. The hum of machinery shifted as the firewall crumbled, releasing a mechanical clank that echoed ominously as gates closed. With a final beep, the security system engaged, sealing them within the confines of the building, trapping them on that level.

"I guess we wait," said Edge as building locked itself down.

Chapter 8

It felt as though hours had passed before a National Guard patrol finally located them inside the tower. Reluctantly, Tucker revealed his CIA credentials, knowing that once the agency received the call for verification, it would escalate straight to the Director. When that confirmation reached him, Director Winford swiftly invoked National Security, ensuring the release of the team along with the bodies of Crawford and Reid.

But now he was back in his Langley office, Tucker grappled with the chaos of the investigation. Two agents lay dead, and another was wounded, all stemming from an operation he had greenlit despite explicit orders to the contrary. This unsanctioned mission had spiraled into a disaster, leaving him at a loss for words when facing the director.

Before departing Homestead, Tucker arranged for a safer place to keep Arslan, particularly in light of Reid's absence. Having witnessed the Order's military prowess, both Tucker and Edge doubted that the Department of Homeland Security building could withstand an attack if the Order decided to target the boy.

Edge had shared with Arslan and explained that they were moving him to a nicer, safer location—one that Tucker and Edge wouldn't know. The only detail they had was that it was a maximum-security safe house, a secret known only to those escorting him. While Arslan was eager for the change, a shadow of disappointment crossed his face at the thought of leaving Edge, Webster, and the others who had kept him in the loop. After some coaxing from Edge, Arslan finally "reluctantly accepted the terms."

As Tucker picked up the lone frame on his desk to study the picture in it, old feelings crept back in. He remembered Reid and Crawford dead; how he gazed at their motionless bodies while they lay on the cold, sterile floor of Global Trust.

Staring at the framed image, *The walls around him stretched and twisted, forming a dark tunnel that seemed to pull him in. A deafening roar filled his ears as the ground trembled beneath him. At the tunnel's end, a blinding light surged forward, growing brighter and consuming the haunting memories of lifeless bodies. He felt as though a spotlight was aimed directly at him, a threat lurking in the shadows. Just as he braced for impact, a familiar voice echoed from the darkness—a voice from his childhood. It pulled him back, yanking him from the tunnel, and suddenly he was seated in his chair, the world around him snapping back into focus.*

Knock, knock.

"Who is it?" Tucker asked, emerging from his thoughts. His gaze lingered on the photograph in the frame. His thumbprint smudged one of the faces, so he wiped it away with the tip of his tie, restoring the image's clarity.

"Edge," he from the other side of the door.

"One second," Tucker responded as he placed the picture back on the desk. "Come on in."

Edge pushed the door open and swept his gaze across the stark room, taking in the unadorned walls. He strolled over to Tucker, his boots thudding softly on the floor, and let his backpack drop with a muted thump beside him.

"I love what you haven't done with the place," Edge mocked.

"Funny," Tucker replied with a dull tone, his enthusiasm drained. He emitted a soft groan as he straightened in his chair.

"How's the body healing?" Edge asked.

"I'm moving. I guess that's saying something."

"Guess that's a negative on the stuntman career?"

Tucker just grimaced and nodded. "I would say so."

They shared a brief laugh together. Edge's laughter came easily, while Tucker's was tight and forced.

"How do you do it?" Tucker asked earnestly.

Edge furrowed his brow, confusion flickering across his face. "Do what exactly?" he asked, uncertain of Tucker's meaning.

"Handle all the shit you've been through?"

"You're talking about Reid and Crawford?" Edge continued.

The names pierced Tucker like a sharp blade. He sensed his grip on composure slipping as his voice rose, "I mean everything. One minute I saw you talking with a kid about cartoons. The next you're slamming your gun into the wound of a soldier to get information. And you act like this is a normal day at the office," he finished, regaining his composure.

"Well, for me it is," Edge responded with a straightforward tone..

Tucker raised his hands in exasperation, emphasizing his point. "That's precisely what I'm talking about!"

Edge studied Tucker, his expression shifting to one of under-standing as he adopted a mentor's tone. "Look, Tucker; you're entering a whole new arena. Your job has protected you from this world. I can't promise you it's going to get easier, but I can promise you that you're going to have more days like this."

"I don't think this world is for me. I mean look, I approve

one unsanctioned operation, and two people are dead, two good agents. I don't have the mindset for this," Tucker protested, his voice wavering as he grappled with the weight of his own doubts, unsure whether he was seeking reassurance from Edge or simply trying to rationalize his own turmoil.

"It comes with being a leader," Edge advised. "You'll have to make decisions that will put people in harm's way. The goal is not to do it wastefully. Crawford and Reid went along knowing what they were getting themselves into. Our job now is to make sure they didn't die in vain. And like it or not you're gonna have to see this through."

"Then how do you keep yourself sane through all this? I mean you've been doing this for a while, and you seem, well... normal."

Edge paused to choose his words carefully, with it being a loaded question he frequently reflected on and had heard from many of the newer team members. "First, you have to believe in what you're doing, that you're working to protect a cause that is just and righteous – in this case, your country – from some imminent peril. If you don't have that kind of belief at your foundation, you're just a mercenary."

"Second," Edge continued, "Understand that your role is warfare, and grasp what that truly entails: it's the final option when all other avenues have failed. Those who wish you harm will stop at nothing to achieve their objectives. It's a matter of life and death between you and them. Don't let their brutality shock you, nor the harsh measures you must take to counter it. Losses are inevitable, and while it doesn't mean you lack compassion or that it won't sting, you must accept that it's part of the reality."

Edge observed as Tucker absorbed every word, the weight of

it settling heavily on him. "If you have any doubts about those two points," he continued, "then this isn't the right path for you."

Tucker rubbed the bridge of his nose. *"Isn't that what I just said,"* he thought. Turning his attention back to Edge, "Doesn't the Geneva Convention fit in there somewhere?"

"I'm referring to the actions you must take in a life-or-death situation, when your very existence hangs in the balance because someone is intent on ending it—whether it's a personal confrontation or a larger conflict. You need to be ready to do whatever is necessary to ensure that you are the one who walks away from it," Edge clarified before he pressed on.

"Third, find peace with your actions and recognize that, despite the terrible things you may have done, you are not a terrible person. This is the toughest challenge. If you start to lose that clarity, it's time to step back. Trust me; I once knew someone who couldn't, and it ruined them."

Tucker fixed his gaze on Edge, "Dear God, you're a philosopher, too."

Edge smiled as Tucker's office phone rang, the sound slicing through the tension. Tucker picked it up with a sigh, bracing himself for bad news. Edge observed him closely, having spent years in the military honing his ability to discern who could endure and who would crumble under pressure.

He recalled a young chalk leader who had lost half his team because of a choice he made under pressure. Faced with two options and no guidance on which was safer, he made a quick decision. No one could have foreseen that it would lead them into a trap. In the aftermath, many senior officials anticipated that the young man would seek a transfer.

Edge saw the same thing in Tucker that he had seen in that

young man. Even though both kept doubting whether they were cut out for the job, that wasn't the root problem bothering them. *"They're both battling their desire for revenge and doing the right thing. But can Tucker separate the two?"* Edge knew the answer to that and, just like the young soldier who returned to the leadership position, he figured Tucker was not leaving anytime soon.

"It looks like the director is ready to see us," Tucker said with little enthusiasm as he placed the phone back on the receiver. "This is going to be fun."

"Just remember Tucker: we made the right call," Edge spoke, striving to bolster his partner's confidence.

"Winford won't see it that way."

"Then we'll have to make it clear to him," Edge replied.

"Good luck with that. Let's see how this plays out for you," Tucker remarked as they stepped out of the office.

****

The elevator doors onto the director's floor slid opened. Tucker tugged at his tie, the fabric feeling constricting yet grounding, a reminder of the professional facade he needed to don. He inhaled deeply, and mentally prepared himself. Beside him, Edge remained effortlessly relaxed in a black polo and jeans, his casual demeanor contrasting sharply with Tucker's rigid formality.

As Tucker neared her desk, he greeted, "Good morning, Mrs. Burton. We have..."

"A meeting with Director Winford, I know," she said, finishing Tucker's sentence. "He's been waiting. He doesn't seem happy by the way, so be prepared," she warned as Tucker grabbed two pieces of candy from the basket on her desk.

"My favorite," Tucker said, unwrapping the caramel treat, offering one to Edge, who politely declined. "As always, thanks for the heads up, Mrs. Burton," he said with a smile.

"Anytime," she replied, her smile brightened by a bold swipe of red lipstick. Her gaze shifted instantly to Edge, curiosity sparking in her eyes. "And who might this be?"

"Excuse me, this is Sergeant Pierce," Tucker replied.

"Glad to meet you, Mrs. Burton." Edge greeted.

"If you ever need anything just let me know. Any friend of Tucker is a friend of mine," she said with a wink before continuing softly. "Don't let me keep you, head right on in."

"Thanks, Mrs. Burton," Tucker said as he walked to the door. Edge nodded and gestured the tipping of a hat.

They stepped into the room, Director Winford stood in front of the grand arched window. His hands were tucked into his pockets, the tension in his posture palpable as he stared out at the sprawling city below.

"Gentlemen, take a seat," Winford said sharply, pivoting to face them. He paused, the silence thickening, reinforcing Mrs. Burton's warning about his mood. "Now, explain what part of waiting until morning you didn't comprehend?"

"Sir, we had viable—" Tucker began.

"Hold it right there," Winford interrupted, his voice sharp. "You've not only ignored my orders but those of the Commander-in-Chief too. Because of your actions, two agents are dead, and one is injured, and you failed to stop the bank robbery. To keep you out of prison, I had to cash in favors that could have been used more effectively."

"It had to be done sir," Edge interjected. "We knew their target, their purpose, and their timing. The amount of money involved was sufficient enough to fund a terrorist organization for a long time and failing to act was not on option."

"Whose idea was it to go in?" Winford asked staring both of them down.

"Mine," they answered simultaneously.

"Cute," he said. "Well, let me start with you, Sergeant Pierce."

"But sir..." Tucker tried to interject.

"Not now agent; you'll get your share of this in a minute. Sergeant, I allowed you in this case to aid Tucker, not to increase the body count. Now, because of you, I have DHS so far up my ass, I feel like a damn sock puppet. You just can't break into a quarantined zone to stop some criminals like a bunch of vigilantes. There's a reason for all the protocols that go on before operations are green lit. And for that very reason, you do not give orders but follow them. I read through your records, the unabridged versions. You and your team are good, but I've noticed the times where you've disobeyed direct orders to complete a mission. Worked out well for you back in Iraq, but not so well in Beijing, huh?"

Edge responded in a level tone of voice. "Sir, Tucker suspected, correctly, that Gamze's murder was part of a larger plan that would ultimately involve military or paramilitary forces. I was brought in to handle such events, and I feel that last night's operation fell within my charter. No one regrets the loss of those two agents more than I do but I stand by my decision to go in."

Winford shot a fierce glare at Edge, who met his gaze with the same.

"This tells me that you're a liability," Winford finally said. "How your commanding officers keep you on is beyond me."

Then he turned his attention to Tucker. "And how the hell, did you let him convince you to go on this chase, let alone approve it?" His tone a mixture of anger and disappointment.

Tucker suppressed the sting of disappointment from someone he respected, burying it deep as he continued to explain. "Sergeant Pierce's logic was sound, and it turned out to be right. When I considered the evidence, I realized it could not go ignored."

"What evidence? That video of Nezaket, a suspected terrorist, mentioning the bank?" Winford asked.

"The video implies that some group, referred to as the 'Order,' was the actual leadership of the plan, not Nezaket," Edge began. "That changed everything because now we're dealing with an organization powerful enough to wipe out an entire city and then obtained enough money to do multiple times over. Yet, the worst part is that we don't know anything about them."

"Where is the video, anyway?" Winford asked.

"I've got a copy of it here, the original in evidence, and another copy in a safe location," Tucker answered, as he reached into his pocket to pull out a small plastic case.

Winford furrowed his brow in confusion. "What's with all the copies?"

Tucker looked to Edge, who nodded. "Sergeant Pierce is of the opinion that the Order has placed or recruited agents within the government that is giving them access to our communications and planning. So we made copies in case the originals came up missing."

"Moles? Rogue agents? That's absurd," Winford scoffed. "And you're buying into that Tucker?" The director chuckled, turning towards his liquor cabinet.

"Not completely, sir, but we have noticed some unsettling

patterns emerging lately," Tucker conceded.

"The Order came for us at the cabin and demanded the video," Edge added. "The fact that we were even there and that the video even existed were both closely held information. They didn't think twice about engaging us so they must have known that we had no backup, which was information that was also closely held."

Winford filled a crystal glass with a generous measure of amber liquid, the rich aroma wafting through the air. It was more than Tucker had ever witnessed him serve himself in one sitting. "When you were breaking into the bank, did you ignore the level of devastation around you? I'd think tracking your location would be easy for people that can bring that much chaos."

"Doesn't mean I'm wrong either," Edge replied, his confidence unshaken by the director's tone.

"We intend to bring this copy to the lab to do a voice analysis of the people in the video," Tucker informed the director. "Our lab has a much larger database of samples to search than the DHS in Florida. If it's someone from one of the agencies, they'll find them," Tucker said as he tapped the box in his hand.

Winford downed the amber liquid in one swift gulp, the warmth spreading through him as he strode back to his desk. He paused, his gaze fixed on a large folder, the corners crumpled and worn, and shook his head slowly, frustration etched across his features. "I must be out of my mind, but it looks like you two are determined to see this through."

He grabbed the folder off his desk and walked it over to Tucker. "Here's the analysis of the missiles. Well, what they've pulled together so far."

Tucker took the folder which could have doubled as a boat

anchor. "*So far?*"

"Uh sir," Tucker began, "I spoke to Agent Xuxa this morning, and she told me it would not be ready until tonight. How did you get this?"

"I'm the Director of Central Intelligence; I can make things happen," Winford said, his voice dripping with sarcasm. "Aside from springing Cowboys from jail, of course. After last night, I planned to pull you both from the investigation and ordered everyone to hold off on sharing any information until I had a chance to speak with you. But after our discussion, it seems passing this off to someone else would be even more foolish than letting you continue," he added before breaking into a fit of coughs.

"Wait, did I hear you right?" Edge asked, perplexed. "You took us off the investigation, and now we're back on it?"

"I'm the Director of Central Intelligence, and it's my job to make those decisions. To be perfectly clear, you and Tucker will continue with this investigation, as long as I say so. Is that understood?"

Tucker and Edge nodded in agreement.

Winford let out a long breath, his shoulders easing slightly. "These last few days have been nothing short of a nightmare for me. In just a couple of hours, I'm expected to brief the President and his cabinet on this entire situation. They're demanding answers, and so am I. That puts the onus on you two to uncover them. Now, get downstairs, speak with Agent Xuxa, and dig up a solid lead on who these bastards are that dared to strike at our homeland."

Tucker turned on his heel, but hesitated, glancing back over his shoulder. "Before we go, I need to ask one last thing. Sir, if we do find anything that we need to act on, we're going to need agents ready to go at a moment's notice. How many men do we have at our disposal?"

"Right now, it's just you and Sergeant Pierce. Bring me something concrete, and I'll ensure action is taken. Until then…" He allowed his voice to fade into silence.

Tucker and Edge exited the director's office and immediately headed for the Department of Technology and Weaponry to speak with Ramona Xuxa. Tucker did not like hearing that they had no other agents to help speed up the process. He and Edge would just have to make do.

"We've done fairly well on our own so far," he thought as he focused on their next instructions to meet with Ramona with a smile. *"There's always a bright side."*

Chapter 9

Tucker and Edge strolled through the corridors of the Technology and Weaponry lab, on a mission to find Ramona Xuxa. In route Tucker explained to Edge that Xuxa was the expert when it came to exotic weaponry, and if anyone had insights into the weapons employed in the Miami attack, it would undoubtedly be her.

As they walked past each lab, Tucker glanced at his reflection in the glass, adjusting and tugging at his tie, ensuring it lay perfectly flat against his collar.

"It's a professional meeting, not a date. We need her expertise, connections, and resources. She is the best the CIA has to offer. Otherwise, I would ask Chad with the Fu Manchu beard," Tucker repeated in his head.

He thought about the number of times he had visited this floor in the past decade he had worked for the agency: the answer was in the low single digits. *"Close to nothing. But now I finally have a good reason to be here."*

Tucker halted in front of the door marked 'Lab 150,' the name mentioned by a colleague they had met earlier. He leaned closer to the glass panel, peering inside to catch a glimpse of the woman at her cluttered desk, completely absorbed in her tasks. As she stretched, lifting her chin to ease the tension in her neck, her glossy black hair cascaded back, unveiling the striking features of Ramona Xuxa. Tucker inhaled sharply, captivated by her undeniable allure.

"You alright man?" questioned Edge.

"What? Oh yeah, I'm fine, just a, just a little warm in the building today, that's all," Tucker said with a laugh as he loosened his tie.

Edge arched an eyebrow, sensing the unease in Tucker's voice. He knew Tucker rarely showed nerves—except when bullets were flying. Having dealt with countless enigmatic personalities, he found Tucker straightforward. He could read him easily and noticed that Tucker's thoughts were clearly drifting elsewhere.

"Yeah," Edge replied, a smirk playing at the corners of his mouth. "Good call on loosening that tie you were fussing over for the past five minutes." He leaned closer to the glass, squinting slightly. "Is that her?"

"Uh, yeah," Tucker said with a hint of fascination, "I mean, yeah, that's her," changing his tone as he saw the expression on Edge's face. "Let's, uh, let's go in," Tucker continued as he took hold of the door handle and pushed.

BLAM!

Tucker's forehead thudded against the glass, a dull ache radiating through his skull. He blinked rapidly, the shock freezing him in place. Ramona glanced up, her laughter ringing out like a melody, bright and infectious.

"*Bad Shakespeare*," Edge thought of the show.

Edge pointed at the door, "Use your key card there, chief."

"Yeah, thanks," Tucker replied, grabbing his card firmly. The beep signaled as the door opened. Tucker entered the room with as much dignity as he could muster.

Ramona gathered her hair into a ponytail as she approached her visitors. The tailored lab coat accentuated her figure, making Tucker question if she could pull off anything. He recognized her dedication to her work, prioritizing skill over looks, yet couldn't help but admire how effortlessly she combined both.

The lab was compact, barely accommodating more than a few people. As Tucker stepped inside, his gaze fell on the counter where Ramona leaned, a vibrant computer screen illuminating her face with a collage of images. Blueprints for missiles sprawled across one side, while snapshots of Miami's skyline and chaotic streets filled the other. Nearby, a chaotic arrangement of books teetered precariously beside folders overflowing with papers, and an assortment of pens lay scattered like soldiers awaiting orders.

"Sorry, I hope I didn't startle you," he apologized, absently rubbing his head.

"Not at all. Actually, I think that door startled *you* by the looks of it," she said with a smile. "So, what brings you to my neck of the woods, Mr. Tucker?"

"Hello, Ramona...I think we can just go with Tucker today," he said.

"You know how it is; force of habit," she said with a smile and a slight shrug. "Anyway, how can I help you, gentlemen?"

"I would like you to meet Sergeant Nicholas Pierce of military intelligence," Tucker introduced.

"Nice to meet you, Sergeant Pierce. I'm Agent Ramona Xuxa. I head up Technology and Weaponry analysis."

"The pleasure is mine," Edge replied.

"Sergeant Pierce is currently working in collaboration with us to track down an organization calling itself the 'Order.'

We suspect they're responsible for what happened in Miami yesterday," Tucker continued, eyes locked on Ramona. "We've run out of leads on our end and were hoping you might have something we can work with. The director gave us your preliminary findings, but we haven't had a chance to read through it yet."

"Frankly, it's a lot of information and time is short. We were hoping you could give us an abridged version," Edge added.

"I had a message sent to me from the Director giving you clearance," Romana said. "Where do you want me to start?"

Edge gestured toward the cluttered computer table. "What can you tell us about the missiles that struck Miami? We noticed in your analysis that you mentioned they weren't typical weapons."

"Yes. Come over here," she said as the group walked over to the tabletop computer.

With deft movements, Ramona placed her hands on the sleek glass surface, her fingers gliding effortlessly as she swept aside the clutter of images. Tucker watched in awe as the pictures cascaded off the bright display, seemingly floating before settling into oblivion. She then expertly centered a blueprint, stretching it wide with a pinch of her fingers, transforming it into a commanding presence that filled the entire tabletop screen.

Edge leaned closer, his brow furrowing as he examined the intricate blue lines on the LCD screen. The weapon displayed was no ordinary piece of technology; it was a mythic creation whispered about among military circles. He had never encountered one in the flesh, but the drawing before him stirred memories of an old sketch he'd stumbled upon, its details now vividly resurrected in front of him.

"Gentlemen, this is the Acoustic Munitions – Pulse/Ballistic missile, or AM-P/B," Ramona stated. "When deployed correctly, it ranks among the most devastating weapons available, second only to nuclear arms. I believe these were used in the Miami attack, but how they fell into the hands of the perpetrators baffles me. These missiles are entirely off the grid; only a few exist. Most military personnel are unaware of their existence, and those who do assume they remain in the experimental stage. It's one of the most classified Black programs."

"I've never come across it, and I've been with the agency for almost ten years," Tucker replied.

"Top Secret Compartmented...and *none* of us would have heard anything about it if our clearance hadn't just been upgraded due to recent events," she explained.

"So, how's it work?" Tucker asked.

"It's a vary complicated system, but to keep it simple. The missile is just the delivery method for the AM-P technology, which causes almost all of the actual destruction. It emits a pattern of acoustic pulses that break down the molecular lattices of metals, non-polymeric materials, and other semi-crystalline materials," Romana explained, glancing slyly at Tucker.

"I'll need a translation of that later," Tucker smiled.

"I hear the whole science bit, but how this thing really cause the destruction it did?" Edge asked.

"Alright, let me simplify this for you. Metals consist of tiny grains that form a crystal-like lattice. These grains bond tightly, providing strength and flexibility. Concrete, on the other hand, is more rigid. AM-P technology targets this granular structure with a sequence of acoustic pulses, causing vibrations that disrupt the bonds between the grains. As a result, metals lose their strength and become malleable, while concrete crumbles into gravel."

"That explains why the buildings in Miami collapsed so quickly," Tucker commented.

Xuxa nodded in agreement. "It would wreak havoc on metal-framed buildings, the backbone of most contemporary skyscrapers. Additionally, the pulses would severely disrupt any electronic devices or electrical systems caught within the blast radius."

"It still seems like it would require a much bigger device to do that much damage," Edge said.

"Do you recall the Seattle earthquake of 2001? That was a test of the AM-P technology's basic function. It was intended to be a minor tremor, barely noticeable, but the program head opted for stronger emissions to ensure accurate readings. He underestimated Seattle's geological volatility. Afterward, seismologists found that the region sits in a rock basin several miles wide, which amplified the acoustic waves from the quake. The outcome? A 6.8 magnitude earthquake and widespread destruction. While it validated the weapon's concept, the program head faced removal for negligence and was reassigned to a base in Greenland, where he now oversees zebra counting. At least that's what I'm told."

"I didn't think there were zebras in Greenland," said Edge.

"Oh, there aren't," Ramona confirmed airily, "so I'm sure he's very bored."

"Humans aren't made of semi-metallic poly-unsaturated whatever, but it seemed to do a number on us," Tucker noted.

"It also works on fluids and since the body is mostly water..." she trailed off.

"How could sound do that kind of damage to a human?" Tucker asked incredulously.

"Ever seen those commercials where a high-fidelity speaker shatters a wine glass? Now, imagine that amplified thousands of times, like the roar of the Saturn V rocket during launch. The sound from those five engines was so intense that anyone caught in the open within a specific radius would have their internal organs crushed and hemorrhaged fatally. That was pure, overwhelming noise, requiring a towering, six-million-pound rocket to produce it. The AM-P/B, however, is a compact, missile-mounted version of this technology. While significantly smaller and more efficient than a rocket, its lethal range remains just as deadly."

"So it hemorrhages the body?" Tucker asked.

"In ways that would have thrilled the Spanish Inquisition," she said, letting the words linger. "The body would be utterly compromised. Victims would become disoriented as the acoustic pulses overwhelmed their inner ear, leading to concussions. Fluids within the body would begin to boil as the acoustic energy transformed into heat. Severe bruising would erupt on the skin as blood vessels ruptured, causing blood to seep from their pores. They would essentially endure the horror of being liquefied alive."

Ramona displayed additional images of the AM-P/B. "The real killer, though, is cardiac arrest. The acoustic pulses disrupt nerve signal transmission, leading the heart into a deadly arrhythmia. If they're fortunate, the victim might lose consciousness before it all comes to an end."

Edge let out a soft laugh, observing Tucker's growing discomfort as Ramona continued to layer on the horrific specifics.

As Ramona finished outlining the gruesome details of the

theoretical death, Tucker felt a lump rise in his throat. "I'm glad I asked. And how long would the process of internal liquefaction take?"

"That depends on how close they are to the warhead. If someone is just a few feet away, they have about ten to fifteen seconds before their heart fails," she explained. "One major drawback of AM-P/B weapons is that their vibrational intensity diminishes with distance. They have a lethal radius of about forty to fifty meters. Within that range, death and destruction are almost guaranteed, but beyond that, the threat decreases rapidly. At around three hundred meters, they can inflict pain, but not lasting harm. In contrast, our standard cruise missiles can strike within five meters of a target. For the AM-P/B to be most effective, it needs to be within roughly two and a half meters."

As she briefed them, Tucker marveled at the depth of her expertise. It became clear how she had ascended to her authoritative role within the agency, particularly as a woman in a male-dominated field. He recalled the whispers around the water cooler, where critics dismissed her achievements as mere advantages of her looks or labeled her as "so smart" that effort was unnecessary. Few acknowledged her intelligence and the relentless dedication she applied to leverage her knowledge.

"The AM-P/B is designed for versatility," she continued. "It can be launched from fixed or mobile platforms on land, at sea, or in the air, striking its target with such stealth that no one even realizes it has been delivered until it happens."

"A good air defense radar would pick it up, right?" Tucker wondered.

"Maybe? The missiles are stealthy, so it's hard to say exactly." With a swift tap on the screen, she paused, and the display shifted seamlessly. A new blueprint emerged, revealing intricate sections of the missile's fuselage, each line and curve meticulously detailed. "It's designed to fly at low altitudes, skimming just above the water's surface. The propulsion system minimizes heat emissions, while the fuselage is crafted to deflect radar signals. Picture a B-2 bomber. If radar systems do detect it, the missile will likely have already struck, as seen in Miami."

Tucker recognized that nuclear weapons carried significant political ramifications, restricting their appeal to terrorists; any group deploying one would face severe repercussions from various fronts. In contrast, these weapons were almost as lethal as a small tactical nuke but could be deployed with far greater ease. On the black market, they posed an entirely new global menace.

"Perfect; devastatingly powerful and effortlessly trans-portable. Just what we want our adversaries to possess," Edge commented. "So, you fire off a bunch of missiles that make buildings sway like they're in a dance and then crumble. It's quite a sight, but conventional weapons already do this and are likely cheaper? What's the advantage here?" Edge asked.

Ramona swiped the blueprint aside, revealing a detailed map of Miami. With a few precise taps on the screen, the image morphed into a network of lines converging on a single point, like veins leading to a heart. "Whoever set off these missiles knew exactly what they were doing. Yes, they took down the other buildings, but the key to this attack was the power plant."

The graphics on the screen were starting to make sense.

"It's the power grid for all of Miami," Tucker thought to himself.

"A nuclear power plant is very solidly built with a pretty stan-dard design for containment purposes. Regular missiles with conventional explosive warheads could knock the plant out, but they may cause only superficial damage. However, when you send in one of these babies, the structural integrity of the plant is completely compromised. The time to return the power plant to operational status changes from weeks to months; maybe even never. As the very fabric of the structure and all its components undergoes transformation at a molecular level."

"So now you harness the advantages of an electromagnetic pulse, but with precision. Like wielding a scalpel instead of a blunt axe," Edge deduced.

"Perhaps, but remember, these weapons have yet to see real-world testing. Miami marks the first documented deployment. Those who acquired these missiles must have had access to extensive test data to understand their capabilities," Ramona stated.

Tucker looked to Edge, who went to open his mouth.

"Don't even think it," Tucker interjected. "I can see it on your face, and I'm already on the same page."

Edge raised his hands in a gesture of surrender, signaling, *"I'm just pointing out, it's overdue."*

Ramona glanced back and forth between them, sensing the silence stretching. When no one spoke up, she decided to take charge of the conversation. "I'm not sure what he has in mind. Someone wants to fill me in," she remarked.

Tucker and Edge exchanged glances, their voices overlapping as they articulated the same thought in distinct phrases.

Ramona raised her hands. "Hold on. One at a time. Sergeant Pierce, since this seems to be your suggestion," she motioned toward him. As Tucker opened his mouth to respond, she quickly silenced him with a finger pressed to her lips.

Edge leaned forward, his voice low. "I suspect there are

government insiders—knowingly or not—assisting this group. The evidence suggests they possess capabilities that go beyond simple phone taps or email hacks. They seem to have near real-time intel, indicating a mole or moles embedded close to the investigation." He crossed his arms, anticipating her rebuttal.

"Then you'll really appreciate this next piece of information," Ramona said, grinning.

"Hey, Tucker, check it out—someone who doesn't think I should be on medication right away!" Edge teased.

Ramona's fingers danced across the table's surface, her focus unwavering. "No, it absolutely makes sense," she replied, her tone steady, "especially considering that this specific weapon was deployed."

While Ramona's attention was momentarily captured by the screen, Edge leaned closer to Tucker, his voice barely above a murmur. "I get why you like her."

Tucker simply pursed his lip and nodded.

The screen flickered, transforming into a map of the United States, gradually honing in on a dense forest in Oregon. "This is where AM-P/P are built."

"All I see are trees," Tucker replied.

"Well, the facility is thirty feet underground. Plus, it's a Black program; you think they're going to let any old satellite pick it up?" She explained.

Edge recalled the covert government facilities he had encountered, each one more clandestine than Area 51, which now felt like a tourist attraction. His sense of astonishment had dulled after discovering a hidden bunker in the Virginia Mountains, a place he frequented with his niece during their hiking trips. "*I swear they are going to run out of places to hide all these things.*"

"How do you know the missiles came from that facility?

We're not the only country working on this technology. We can't be," Edge stated.

"I can confirm we're not the only ones developing this technology, but we are the furthest along. Given specific circumstances, you could say we've completed it. Additionally, the missile designs used in Miami are exclusive to that facility."

"So how does this tie into my 'conspiracy theory?'" Edge wondered.

"This facility is so top secret that the list of people who know about it is tiny, even by Black program standards, and even fewer know what they are making."

As Edge's theory unfolded, it became increasingly clear that it was the only viable explanation. The thought of individuals with such high-level clearance plotting against their own country unsettled Tucker deeply.

"So, you're on that list?" Tucker asked.

"Me? That the facility existed? Yes. As for what it made: no, not until a day ago. I am now cleared to know what I've told you, but the deepest details of how it works are in compartments way beyond any clearance I'm ever likely to have," Ramona answered.

"Even you?" Tucker asked, surprised.

"They only lifted the veil barely enough for us to do our job," she replied.

"Odd that the warhead and the missile were built in the same facility," Edge observed. "Usually, they're built in separate places and only assembled at an ops base at mission go time. Who's running the place?"

Edge anticipated a response that would point to the Air Force due to the missile or the Army because of the AM-P technology. Ramona's reply caught him off guard.

"Believe it or not, a private company operates the facility. It masquerades as a lumber yard, serving as a clever front. The Defense Advanced Research Projects Agency contributed some funding for the AM-P development, while the CIA covered the rest, yet it remains privately managed. This means we have not only your rogue agent scenario but also a workforce composed largely of civilians. Although these civilian employees undergo extensive background checks, the involvement of government personnel renders those checks practically useless. It's a highly secure setup disguised as an innocuous civilian operation, creating a security nightmare for anyone astute enough to notice," Ramona explained.

"Edge," Tucker urged, his voice intense, "we need to head there. It's our only lead, and I'm certain we'll uncover a link to the Order."

Edge nodded in agreement.

"If there's a mole, they might anticipate our discovery of the facility and set a trap," Edge pointed out. "It's happened before." He noticed Tucker processing that unsettling thought, the weight of their previous conversation evident in his expression.

"We don't have a choice," Tucker said, just as Edge had expected.

"However, there's a hitch," Ramona interjected.

"What's that?" Tucker asked, refocusing on her.

"They aren't going to just let you stroll into the facility, even with the highest clearance."

"So how do we gain access?" Edge inquired.

"Well, I *am* one of few people with a clearance that—"

"Nope! Not happening!" Tucker snapped, cutting her off. "We've tangled with these guys a couple of times already, and they are top-notch tough. And given the likelihood that this is a trap, the threat level is too high. We've already lost two good men to them. You are too important to this case to lose on a recon mission."

"I understand this isn't ideal, but hear me out," Ramona urged. "Gaining entry to a facility like this is just the beginning. Once inside, the environment is highly regulated. Strict protocols must be adhered to. From my visits to similar sites, I've realized that you essentially need to communicate in a specific jargon unique to each location."

"We'll have to pose as an inspection team," she said, her tone firm. "We'll need a letter from the director that includes the right 'flag words' for authentication. For instance, if we enter a nuclear weapons facility, we must use the Pinnacle flag word. With those credentials, they're obligated to let us in and respond to our inquiries. However, our ability to ask questions will be limited: some topics are safe, while others will raise red flags. If they suspect us, they'll still answer, but it could be misleading. No offense," she added, glancing at Edge, "but I doubt you have the experience to recognize when you're being fed nonsense. So, I'll lead as the expert, and you two will take on the investigator roles. That's the only way we'll get in."

Edge met Tucker's gaze, sensing his reluctance. "She's right. We need her with us."

"I understand the risk believe me," said Ramona. "But if there's a connection between Miami and the AM-P/B facility then I need to know."

"No offense Ramona, but I still don't think this is a good idea. Edge, come on; you know the people we're up against," Tucker responded.

"The country has just been attacked, and that facility might hold the answers," Ramona insisted. "I'm going, and the question is whether you'll come with me. How do you expect to secure clearances on such short notice without my assistance?"

Tucker pressed his back against the cold, unyielding wall, his gaze fixed on the scuffed floorboards beneath his feet. Each word from Ramona felt like a tightening noose, constricting his choices until only one remained—the very path he had hoped to sidestep.

Edge raised his eyes to Tucker and reaffirmed, "So, what's the call?"

Reluctantly, Tucker exhaled deeply. "Fine, against my better judgment, when do we head out?"

"I'll leave that decision to you. Based on what you've shared, it should happen sooner rather than later," Ramona replied.

"I suggest we leave first thing tomorrow morning," Edge offered. "That gives us time to make arrangements and prep for departure."

Edge glanced back and forth between them, searching for any signs of dissent, but silence reigned.

"Ramona, collect all the materials you need for the facility clearance. Brief us on their operations. In the meantime, I'll speak with Director Winford to finalize our flight from Langley for tomorrow. I'll update you with the departure time once it's set," Tucker said assuredly.

"Alright," she replied, a newfound confidence lifting her posture slightly.

"Tucker, we need to move," Edge urged, pivoting to Ramona shaking her hand. "It's been a pleasure meeting you, and I'm glad to have you with us."

"Likewise," she said with a smile. "And might I say, I love that call sign; *Edge.* It's unique."

Edge gave her a smile, and a thumbs up in agreement as he turned to leave. Walking out of the lab, he looked back and saw Tucker walking towards Ramona. *I'll give him a minute.*

Tucker faced Ramona, his expression serious. "I believe you can handle this. It's not your skills I doubt; it's the risks involved in this case."

"I understand your concerns, but I have my own responsibilities to fulfill," she responded.

"I understand," taking a few steps towards the door he added, "Thank you for the information and I'll talk to you later," Tucker ended.

"Tucker," she said with a smile, locking eyes with him. "You're welcome."

He smiled back, then turned to rejoin Edge. As he rounded the corner and disappeared from view, she refocused on her tasks.

Tucker pressed the elevator button, feeling Edge's grin without needing to glance over. "What's got you in such a good mood?" he asked.

"I think you were more nervous going into that lab then you were going to the bank last night," Edge said.

"No," Tucker replied, shaking his head. "I just haven't used those doors in ages; I forgot I needed the key," he admitted, his gaze fixed on the elevator's call button.

"It's okay. She feels the same way," Edge pointed out as they stepped onto the elevator.

"I have no idea what you mean," Tucker insisted, his thoughts igniting with the possibility that Ramona might feel the same way. "We're just colleagues, nothing beyond that," he added.

"Alright, you don't need to persuade me any further," Edge

said, raising his hands in surrender. Tucker chose a floor, and they stood in silence as the doors began to close.

As the elevator doors slid shut, Edge turned to Tucker and asked, "What did you think of that cat necklace she wore?"

"It's a sparrow," Tucker quickly corrected, only to realize he had stepped into a trap.

Edge's satisfied grin was unmistakable in the elevator door's reflection.

"You're right, only a good co-worker would notice that," Edge ended.

Chapter 10

The light to their elevator stopped on the seventh floor.

"What's your next move," Edge asked as Tucker took his first step off the elevator.

"What? You're not coming with me to throw the pitch to Winford?" Tucker asked, looking back at him.

"Not this time," Edge replied, blocking the elevator door with his hand. "I need to return to my hotel to pick up a few essentials and get ready for tomorrow. I won't be caught off guard again. You can handle the director on your own. I'll see you later."

"Stay sharp out there," Tucker warned as the elevator doors slid shut. He lingered for a moment, tapping the file he carried against his palm before making his way to his office. Upon entering, he found it just as he had left it: tidy and still. After spinning a pen between his fingers and surveying the room, he finally picked up the desk phone to make the call.

"Hello, Director. This is Tucker."

"Tucker, you just seem to have this intuition about you," Winford greeted.

"What do you mean by that sir?"

"It means that you seem to know when I am in the middle of something because that's the only time you call," the Director said before erupting into a steady stream of coughing.

"Sir I know it's none of my business, but you might want to get that cough looked at."

"Well, when you're my age you'll understand that coughing becomes a part of daily life. Now are you going to worry about my health or are you going to tell me about this problem?"

Leaning forward in his chair Tucker summarized the situation, "Sir we found the facility that made the missiles, and we need you to get our clearance to enter and find out how they were used against us."

"How am I supposed to get you access to another country's facility—" the director began to question before Tucker interrupted.

"It's us, sir. The weapons are being developed in a secret facility in Oregon."

"So now you're telling me that we bombed ourselves. I find that a little hard to swallow."

"I doubt that we bombed ourselves," Tucker amended. "We're pretty sure that the technology was either stolen or purchased on the black market somehow. That's why I'm calling. I need transport for Sergeant Pierce, Agent Xuxa, and myself for tomorrow," he said, juggling the pen back and forth between his fingers, awaiting Winford's reaction.

"Okay, how sure are you that the weapon is from this non-existent facility, in Oregon of all places?" Winford's voice came across calm and collected. His lack of urgency bothered Tucker.

"Agent Xuxa reviewed the missile data from Miami, and it aligns with our designs, not those from foreign nations," Tucker stated, listening to Winford's persistent cough in the background.

"Why haven't I heard about this facility before?" Winford continued.

"Sir I just learned of it myself."

"When do you plan to ship out?"

"I am aiming for, o'seven hundred tomorrow morning."

"And why do you need my help? You're the lead investigator of a major attack on the US."

Winford absorbed Tucker's explanation of Ramona's reasoning and the signed letters she required from him as Director. He couldn't deny Tucker's resolve; he was pushing ahead with remarkable speed.

"That's why I chose him," Winford thought.

"Okay," Winford agreed, "Everything will be ready for you and your people by five hundred. When you return, I will need a full report as to what's going on. If the President comes down on me, believe me, you will feel it as well."

"Understood, sir."

"Okay son, catch the son of bitches," Winford said, clearing his throat. "Time is of the essence!"

"Will do sir," Tucker ended placing the phone in the cradle.

****

Edge paused by a weathered pay phone, its metal casing gleaming under the flickering streetlight. He pressed the worn buttons with practiced ease, each digit a reminder of past conversations. The phone rang, the sound echoing in the stillness of the night, until a gravelly voice responded on the other end.

"Hello," Doom answered.

"Hey buddy, it's Nick. How are things by you?"

"Been busy fixing up the house. Damn porch railing rotted out. How are things on your end?"

"We'll talk later, but for now, I need you to get in touch with Pitch and Trident. I need some help with that gig in D.C. that I told you about."

"This is about Miami?" Doom asked curiously.

"That clear huh?" Edge responded. He could almost see Doom nodding slowly, a knowing expression crossing his face. "I'm going to send you a secure message with what I need you guys to do."

"What about the rest of the team?"

"No need at the moment. The three of you should be enough. You guys are just my precaution."

"The wife is not going to like me leaving so early, but I gotcha," Doom remarked.

"Tell her that I'll make it up to her," Edge promised.

"She'll expect you to keep that promise," Doom chuckled. "Catch you later, Nick."

"See ya bro," Edge finished as he placed the phone on the receiver. With his hands tucked into his pants pockets, he paused for a moment, scanning the street. Satisfied that everything appeared as it should, he stepped forward, disappearing into the shadows of the night.

Chapter 11

The helicopter blades whirred to silence on the helipad, Tucker, Edge, and Ramona stepped onto the rugged terrain of southern Oregon. Below, the valleys unfurled like a living canvas, sunlight spilling over the emerald hills in vibrant hues reminiscent of an Albert Bierstadt masterpiece. Tucker paused, inhaling the crisp air, his gaze lingering on the tranquil landscape. A flicker of longing crossed his mind for a life filled with more moments like this.

Tucker's peaceful moment shattered as his eyes caught three figures in dark suits, leaning against two rugged hardtop jeeps parked thirty yards away on the tarmac. Their watchful gazes screamed authority. A jolt of panic surged through him. *"Damn! How did they find us?"*

Tucker squinted, noting the casual slouch of the men, hands tucked into pockets or arms crossed casually over their chests. Reid's words echoed in his mind: reading people was half the battle. These three, with their relaxed stances and unhurried demeanor, didn't radiate immediate danger; at least for now, they seemed more attentive than hostile.

"Who are those guys?" Ramona inquired, articulating the very thought swirling in Tucker's mind.

"I was wondering that myself," he admitted.

Both pairs of eyes turned toward Edge, who walked stood, his expression unreadable.

"You guys wait here," Edge instructed, his voice steady as he began descending the helipad staircase, making his way toward the trio of men waiting by the jeeps.

"I'll come with you," Tucker said, following.

"No, stay here with Ramona," Edge repeated, raising a hand to emphasize the command. "I Got this buddy."

"Something's not right," Tucker thought.

As Edge approached the trio, the gravel crunched beneath his boots, sending tiny stones skittering. The tall man, casually leaning against the jeep, lifted his chin in acknowledgment, his eyes flickering toward Tucker and Ramona. A slight nod accompanied his gaze, as if assessing their presence before returning his focus to Edge.

Frustration simmered within Tucker as he watched Edge stride toward the men, feeling the weight of exclusion press down on him. With Ramona at his side for this field operation, he couldn't shake the unease that came from being kept in the dark.

"Why didn't Edge introduce them if he knew who they were? If he was aware they'd be here, why hadn't he mentioned it to us? And if he didn't know them, what compelled him to approach them so confidently?" The questions churned in Tucker's mind, each one more unsettling than the last.

"Do you know what's going on here?" Ramona asked.

"Not the slightest, but I intend to find out," Tucker promised, as he made his way down the stairs.

As they approached, and before Tucker could get a word out. Edge plastered a broad, inviting smile across his face, extending his arm in a welcoming gesture toward the trio of men. "Tucker,

Ramona, I would like for you to meet part of my Delta team; this is Doom, Pitch, and Trident."

Ramona stood closest to Doom, her hand reaching out in a confident gesture. "It's a pleasure to meet you," she said, her voice steady as she introduced herself.

Doom remained silent, straightening to his towering height before nodding and slowly reaching out his hand. Ramona couldn't shake the impression that his deliberate movements resembled tectonic plates shifting beneath the earth. As his massive hand enveloped hers, a flicker of apprehension coursed through her; men of his stature often lacked awareness of their own strength. To her surprise, his grip was firm yet surprisingly gentle.

Pitch flashed a warm smile, his eyes crinkling at the corners as he extended a hand. "Pleasure to meet you," he said, his voice smooth and inviting.

Trident grasped her hand, his words a low murmur that slipped past her ears, indistinct and unclear.

"Trident, a little clarity wouldn't hurt," Pitch suggested with a chuckle. Turning to Ramona, he added, "Don't mind Mr. Manners; he's usually chattier, especially around women. As for our strong, silent friend," he said, gesturing toward Doom with a thumb, "his personality is only marginally more engaging than his call sign."

"Pleasure to meet you," Tucker said, locking eyes with each of the three men in turn. "Edge, could we have a moment alone?" He gestured slightly away from the group, his tone firm yet discreet.

"Sure. I'll be right back, guys," Edge said.

Once they were out of earshot, Tucker turned to Edge, his voice low but charged with urgency. "What's really happening here?"

"I figured we could use the help," Edge answered.

"Are you holding out on me? If you've got information, now's the time to share it. If we're going to take these guys down, I need every detail you have," Tucker snapped, frustration lacing his words.

"I told you I wasn't going to be caught off guard again. So, I called in a favor to lend a hand, should the shit hit the fan again."

"But why the secrecy?"

"I was testing a theory," Edge said, unemotionally.

Edge's terse replies were starting to irritate Tucker. *"I don't have time for this,"* he wanted to snap, but refrained with the others nearby. "And what exactly is this theory?" he asked instead.

Edge held Tucker's gaze, the weight of the moment stretching between them. After a beat, he delivered the words with unyielding clarity, "You're compromised."

****

As Tucker and Edge moved away, Ramona lingered near Doom, Pitch, and Trident, arms crossed and her briefcase resting against her leg. Her gaze drifted to Tucker, captivated by the way his jacket fluttered in the brisk mountain wind as he strode forward. There was something about him that sparked her curiosity. Sure, she had noticed his endearing awkwardness around her before, but during this trip, a new layer had emerged—one that revealed a quiet confidence, a strength that drew her in.

Snapping back to the present, she turned to her companions

and inquired, "What do you think is going on over there?"

Trident tilted his head slightly in Tucker and Edge's direction. "Looks like he didn't waste any time."

All eyes shifted to Tucker, who gestured animatedly, his frustration evident in every sweeping motion of his arms. In stark contrast, Edge remained composed, his hands tucked casually into his pockets.

"That's gotta be a record," Pitch commented.

"You know how suits are," Trident added, "and you know the Sarge doesn't hesitate to call 'em out."

"What's that supposed to mean?" Ramona asked, clearing her throat.

"No offense, Agent Xuxa, but Spec Ops and suits simply don't mix," Pitch explained.

"You can say that again," Trident added. "Man, he looks pissed."

"Doesn't he look familiar to anyone?" asked Pitch.

"You're slipping," Doom replied. "That's that analyst, Dante Tucker, from Nightwolf."

"Name rings a bell."

Pitch raised his eyebrows. "Wow, it's been a long time. He looks…"

"Taller," Trident finished.

Ramona bristled at the way they seemed to mock Tucker, irritation bubbling beneath the surface. She sensed an urge to defend him, though she struggled to pinpoint exactly what she was defending—his dignity, perhaps, or the quiet strength he had begun to reveal.

"To set things straight," she began, "The fact that you can joke that Tucker wants people getting killed on his watch is unacceptable. The victims in Miami are very much on his mind, along with the lost DHS agents."

"Hell, if that doesn't sound like someone we know," Doom said slowly.

"Anyway, what are they talking about, Doom?" Trident asked, abruptly changing the conversation.

Doom glanced toward Tucker and Edge, his brow furrowing slightly. "I can't make out what Sarge saying," he said, keeping his tone ambiguous as he turned to Ramona. "But that suit is firing off a lot of questions."

"And how do you know that?" Ramona asked, mildly frustrated that it felt as though they were conversing in a dialect entirely foreign to her.

After a brief pause, Doom finally spoke, "Spending hours peering through a scope has imparted many lessons. One of those skills is the knack for reading lips."

****

"What do you mean by 'compromised'?" Tucker demanded, his voice strained as he fought the urge to raise it. He was certain Edge had a rational explanation, yet the sharp sting of being implicated in the problem felt like a bitter pill lodged in his throat.

"Consider this: every time you provide an update on our investigation, the Order seems to track us down, strike, and come perilously close to finishing us off," Edge explained.

Tucker crossed his arms, irritation bubbling beneath the surface. "Honestly, it's not surprising. After encountering them, I wouldn't be shocked if they've already hacked my phone like I mentioned earlier," he said, frustration lacing his tone. "That doesn't mean I'm compromised; for all we know, they could have your phone tapped as well."

Edge's face remained impassive. "That's accurate, but I didn't make any calls before we headed to the tower." He observed Tucker as he mulled over the statement. "And it's not about the phone; you've switched devices so many times, even using landlines they might think you'd rely on, that the chances of them monitoring every phone you've used for updates are slim. The only constant is the recipient of your messages."

"So, you think the mole is someone I've been talking to? Come on! The only person I've called about this was—" Tucker stopped as he realized the implication.

Edge nodded as Tucker came to the realization.

Tucker's anger flared—first at the slight against his boss, and second at the impossibility of reconciling the two conflicting truths. "Hold on. So, you're trying to tell me that a Vietnam vet, long time patriot, and Director of the CIA is behind the Order? I could agree with your paranoia about rogue organizations, but this is too much. There's no way he's involved," Tucker denied.

"Come on Tucker, use that intelligent brain of yours and put it together," Edge prompted. "Every single time we advised Winford of our plans, the Order showed up. For Christ sakes, he, Reid and Webster, were the only ones that knew we were going to the cabin, besides the kid. Reid's dead and Webster's wounded. I doubt they were working for them. I didn't tell you about bringing in my team so that you couldn't tell him in case I'm right. That way, if the Order does show up, we have an advantage. And if he's not behind this then we have nothing to worry about."

The idea that Winford could be the enemy rattled Tucker deeply. He had always regarded Winford with utmost respect, and if Edge was right, it meant he would have to completely reassess his beliefs, much like evaluating a house's stability after a quake.

"If, and I do mean *if*, your assumptions are correct, why would a man who has received both the Congressional Medal of Honor and the Purple Heart for his military actions, who practically rebuilt the CIA, do something like this?" Tucker asked.

"Not sure about that yet," Edge admitted. "But remember, you serve the office of the DCI, not the man in it. You may admire the man in the position now, but men have faults, and sometimes they change. Either way, I know that's something you'll figure out," Edge said, placing a firm hand on Tucker's shoulder. "Collect your evidence for now and we'll bring in all those responsible, no matter who it is. The important thing is not allowing your emotions to interfere with your judgment. Understood?"

"Yeah, I gotcha," Tucker replied, calming down. He was frustrated, but Edge had a point; they needed to resolve this later. Right now, their priority was the missile facility.

Tucker paused a second to get his thoughts together while Edge returned to the group. He couldn't look unbalanced around them, although he figured they probably already saw his reaction. "*Whiskey, Tango, Foxtrot,*" he repeated the mantra in his head before as he rejoined the group.

"Ramona," Edge called as he neared her, "my team will be joining us at the facility. I realize their clearances aren't in order, but we don't have time to sort that out. We need you to get us in. If the Order has more weapons, those clearances won't matter."

"Don't worry Sergeant, clearances won't be a problem," she responded.

"Now that the family reunion has wrapped up, let's hit the

road," Tucker said, forcing himself to set aside thoughts of Winford for now. He was ready to push the investigation ahead.

"He's right," Edge said, nodding. "It's good to talk, but the Order won't pause for us. I'll debrief you three more in route." He pulled a map from his coat pocket and scanned it. "There are a few rest stops before we reach the facility. We can stop at one to finalize our plan. I just want to keep our strategy out of sight."

"Sounds good to me," Tucker agreed.

Without any further dissent, Edge tucked the map away into his pocket. "Time to get moving."

****

While navigating the winding roads of Siuslaw National Forest, Tucker struggled to focus on their urgent mission—the investigation of the sawmill that had been repurposed into a missile factory. Yet, more pressing than the task at hand was the presence of Ramona beside him, surrounded by breathtaking scenery that felt almost surreal. The urge to express his feelings for her surged within him, an impulse that seemed impossible to ignore.

"It's beautiful isn't it," she said.

"My words exactly," Tucker mused, glancing at her as she admired the view from the passenger window. "Yeah, it's amazing how places like this still exist," is what he said aloud.

He stole a glance at her, momentarily at a loss for words. There was an undeniable allure to a woman in a business suit, particularly when that woman was Ramona Xuxa.

"I wish I could escape to places like this more often. There's something about the beauty here that makes the chaos of the world fade away," she confessed, her gaze drifting back to the vibrant greens and blues outside the window.

With each conversation, Tucker discovered their shared perspectives and interests. He realized he needed to find a way to arrange more outings like this.

"It really does have a way of washing everything else away," Tucker replied, his voice softening. "It feels like nothing else exists in this moment. I could easily lose myself in this place for hours."

"Please don't get lost. I would like to find this place before the Order does," Edge said from the back seat.

"Edge, after we hit the rest stop, how about you go chaperone your bros in the other jeep?" Tucker said with a smile.

"Ooh! Testy, testy," Edge teased, as Ramona laughed lightly.

"Don't worry Edge, we're still on track," Tucker assured him. "According to the map, we're just shy of a half hour-ish-ness."

"Very precise, Mr. Analyst," Ramona commented.

"Yeah, well I'm not exactly Mr. Tracker," Tucker replied as the map was snatched out of his hand.

"Thankfully, I am," Edge asserted. "The signs say there's a rest stop a few miles up the road. Why don't we stop there, do a little planning."

Tucker brought the vehicle to a stop at the desolate rest area, dust swirling in the air as Doom, Pitch, and Trident parked their SUV behind him. Edge adjusted his reflective sunglasses, scanning the lot for any lurking threats. His gaze landed on four bright blue port-o-potties standing like sentinels in the distance, while the rhythmic tapping of a woodpecker echoed through the trees. Satisfied that they were alone, he relaxed slightly, confident in their privacy.

Tucker swung open the back door and retrieved his weathered

brown leather bag, its surface worn from countless missions. He strolled to a nearby picnic table, the wood rough against his fingertips. Setting the bag down, he unzipped it and pulled out his laptop, the metallic click of the lid echoing in the stillness. He laid a photo flat on the table, its edges slightly frayed, and the others gathered around, leaning in to catch a glimpse of the image over his shoulder.

"Okay, here's how this all started," Tucker spelled out. "Approximately six days ago this man," Tucker pointed to a picture of Gamze, "was assassinated, in his cabin in an isolated area of the Everglades."

"Is that who I think it is?" asked Pitch.

"Sure is," answered Trident.

"Gamze Nezaket," Tucker confirmed. "CEO of Turkish Petroleum Incorporated. Given that he is no longer amongst the living, we can't question him. We believe he had a hand in the Miami bombings; he wasn't the mastermind but a facilitator in some capacity for an, until recently, below-the-radar organization called the 'Order'."

"That's it, they couldn't come up with something that's not cliché," Trident murmured to Pitch, "But, yet catchy."

Tucker pressed on, "The missiles involved in the attack were manufactured at the facility ahead. Our mission is to enter the building and figure out how a few of them disappeared and fell into the Order's hands without anyone noticing."

Doom rubbed the back of his neck, glancing at the road signs that lined their path. "Looks like the only thing up ahead is a logging company," he said, his brow furrowing in confusion.

"Well, it seems the cover operation is functioning as intended," Ramona remarked, her fingers deftly navigating the laptop to pull up the blueprints. "The logging company serves merely as a façade for what's hidden forty feet beneath the surface: two hundred and thirty acres devoted to the development of AM/P-B technology." She turned the screen toward the group, revealing a detailed layout of the facility for all to examine.

"Shit, all that's underneath these mountains?" Trident asked in astonishment, summing up everyone's thoughts. "Pardon, my French."

"Indeed, everything you see above is just a cover for what lies beneath these mountains, and it's secured more rigorously than Fort Knox," Ramona explained, her tone serious. "The facility comprises four distinct sections: living quarters, administrative offices, laboratories, and the manufacturing floor, which takes up the bulk of the space. Both civilian workers and US military personnel are active within its walls."

"And who is this facility director?" Trident asked.

"That would be a man by the name of Randolph Quinn," she replied.

"What do we have on him?" Edge asked.

"He served just shy of two years in the Navy. There are whispers that his overprotective parents pulled some strings to get him discharged early, claiming the military was too perilous for their precious son, especially with the war raging. After that, he seamlessly transitioned into the role of Director, and now he embodies everything a bureaucrat is—completely entrenched in civilian life," Ramona explained.

"So, he's an over privileged slacker," Pitch summed up bluntly.

"You could put it that way," Ramona agreed.

"And who are his over-connected parents?" Edge inquired.

"You must have heard of Senator Madeline Quinn of Texas

and her husband, Governor Ken Quinn?"

"Fraid not," Edge refuted.

"Well, let's just say money isn't an issue for them," Ramona continued.

"So, this is a civilian facility?" Pitch asked.

"Yes, it's technically a civilian facility, but that doesn't stop Uncle Sam from implementing security throughout."

"And by security you mean Military Police,' right?" Pitch questioned back.

"From what I read, the procedures for hiring are standard military, but for staffing the military provided candidates and Quinn was given a choice of who to hire," Edge explained.

"Oh, that's not too shabby," Pitch remarked, letting his arms fall to his sides in a more casual stance.

Tucker furrowed his brow, uncertainty flickering across his face. "How do you figure? They're all trained military personnel."

"Yeah, but they're employed by a private manufacturing firm," Trident interjected, his tone laced with skepticism. "Not a legitimate security agency that's subject to regular audits. They've probably grown complacent, out of shape, and sluggish. The most excitement they've had in years is from online gaming marathons. They won't pose much of a challenge; I could easily take this place down all on my own."

"Now, what are the odds the Order knows that?" Tucker asked looking to Edge.

"Hence the backup," he replied gesturing to his team. "Okay everyone, time's a-wasting."

Tucker and Ramona made their way back to the vehicle, while Edge lingered behind, preparing to deliver a final briefing to his team.

"They're on their way," Edge declared, his voice steady yet urgent. "I'm absolutely sure of it. They're armed to the teeth. Our mission is to safeguard any intel we uncover, as well as them," he gestured toward Tucker and Ramona, "and let's not forget about the innocent bystanders who might find themselves in harm's way."

"Well damn, man, I thought you were going to give us something hard. Packed my good sidearm for nothing," Doom joked.

"They're planning on us being here," Edge reiterated. "This is where they can make us disappear. They've failed twice so far because they underestimated us and we got lucky, but two good men died in the process. I don't think they're going to go surgical this time. They're going to scorch the earth."

"They better be careful what they wish for," Trident said, fixing his glasses.

"My thoughts exactly. See ya there," Edge finished.

The group dispersed. As Edge walked to the car, he looked at Tucker, who was reading the map. "*I hope you learned something in those battles,* he thought to Tucker. *You're gonna need it today.*"

Chapter 12

The path to the lumberyard resembled a slender ribbon winding through the woods. Despite being dirt, it was surprisingly even underfoot, its surface firm and compact. Towering trees leaned inwards, their branches intertwining overhead, casting a cool gloom that swallowed the trail in darkness. From above, it vanished entirely, hidden among the dense sea of green, with only the main road visible far off, leading to a small clearing deep within the unyielding forest.

After driving along, a single road for what felt like an eternity, the cramped team finally arrived at the facility. Nestled in a clearing a few hundred yards across, it embodied the essence of a lumber mill. The sole oddity in the scene was the imposing twelve-foot-high electric fence, its top lined with menacing razor wire, encircling the entire property.

"If this place is a lumberyard, then it must be home to the priciest timber on the planet," Tucker mused, his voice echoing in the stillness around him.

Tucker eased the vehicle to a halt at the gate, where two men emerged from the booth, their thick plaid shirts and worn blue jeans blending into the rugged surroundings. One strode purposefully toward the car, while the other leaned against the doorframe, his right arm propped casually yet revealing the subtle bulge of body armor beneath his clothing.

Edge's gaze flicked to the man leaning against the booth, his fingers resting on a small emergency switch, a detail that hinted at the seriousness of their surroundings. A few other figures drifted into view, their voices low as they gathered around crates stacked haphazardly, the shapes within casting ominous shadows that suggested a cache of weapons—yet another layer of security woven into the atmosphere.

"Mornin'. What can I do for ya?" asked the man with a warm smile, as Tucker rolled down his window.

Ramona reached across Tucker, extending her credentials to the guard. "Good morning. I'm Agent Ramona Xuxa with the CIA. I need to speak with Mr. Quinn. Here's my clearance."

The man's demeanor changed from folksy to polite but aloof. "State your business, please."

"Inspection. National Security. These men and those in the vehicle behind me are part of my team and they are here to help collect information for the inspection."

"Okay, Agent Xuxa. Wait here, please."

The guard returned to the booth and picked up the phone. After a moment, he returned. "Mr. Quinn is expecting you, Agent Xuxa. A squad will be driving by in a moment; follow it to the entrance. Once there you will be escorted further into the facility by appointed personnel."

A sharp buzzer echoed through the air, and the heavy gate creaked open, the guard gesturing them forward with a nod. "Thank you, sir," she replied, flashing her trademark reassuring smile, a practiced expression honed over countless months of navigating the complexities of her role at the agency.

"Enjoy your visit, ma'am," the second guard said as they passed.

As the guard had indicated, a burly man on an ATV appeared before them, motioning for them to follow. His muscular arms, reminiscent of tree trunks, hinted at a strength that could easily uproot a sapling. A tattoo of the Army Ranger's emblem adorned his forearm, a badge of honor etched into his skin. With a broad grin, he waved enthusiastically before revving the engine and guiding them off down the path.

"Wow, they're committed to their roles out here," Tucker commented as he started the game of following the leader.

Entering onto a large, graveled lot, Tucker felt uneasy as he watched the gates close behind them in the rearview mirror. *"What I'm I worried about? I guess I've been spending too much time around Edge, starting to think like him,"* he thought.

"Does anyone find this odd?" Edge asked, suspicious. "They didn't ask who Tucker, and I were, let alone the three others in the next car. If this facility is as secret as you say, I would expect them to at least ask for IDs from everyone and search the vehicles, White House style."

"You got that gut feeling thing going on again?" Tucker inquired, sensing Edge's tension echoing his own.

"Make fun of the gut, but it's gotten me through a lot; everything from close call ambushes to my great aunt's casserole. The thought of that taste still makes me nauseous."

"Close call in those ambushes?" Ramona asked.

"Yeah, but that casserole left the more serious scars," he continued, prompting a wave of laughter that rippled through the group, easing the tension in the air.

A few hundred yards past the gate, the team arrived at a sprawling turning circle. Towering stacks of lumber loomed like silent sentinels, each awaiting its turn to be transformed. The ATV came to a halt before the central one of three massive, prefabricated buildings. A weathered star, emblazoned with a bold red number two, hung above the entrance.

"Would you look at this," Pitch said stepping out of the car looking around. "Looks like this place is still operational," he said as the car doors thudded shut behind him.

The lumberyard sprawled before them, dominated by three colossal Quonset huts that dwarfed anything they had encountered. Each structure, half the length of a football field, bore the scars of time—rust streaked across their corrugated surfaces, whispering tales of years spent in the elements. Within the two outer huts, towering stacks of lumber reached heights of fifteen to twenty feet, meticulously cut and arranged, ready to embark on their journey to distant destinations.

"That's because it is still operational. Employs nearly a hundred workers; a very large operation for this area," Ramona answered.

Edge surveyed the lumberyard's layout, absorbing every detail. He had encountered numerous covert government facilities, but this one was unparalleled—an entire complex concealed beneath a fully functioning lumberyard. It was clear why the cover was so effective.

"How long has this place been operational again?" Tucker asked.

"Sixty-three years to be exact," a male voice answered beside them.

Everyone turned to locate the voice's owner, revealing a middle-aged African American man clad in khaki pants sharply creased as if freshly pressed. His brown boat shoes bore the wear of countless miles, suggesting he had trekked through a desert. Small, round-rimmed glasses perched on his broad nose, amplifying his nerdy charm. Stubble adorned his face, gray hairs mingling with those atop his head, indicating he hadn't shaved in days. Despite this, his solid arms filled out the short sleeves of his button-down flannel shirt, showcasing a surprising strength.

Ramona's eyes opened wide when she heard the voice.

"I'm Doctor—," he began.

"Collins," Ramona finished, with a touch of awe in her voice.

"Yes, I am. How do you know that young lady?" he asked.

"I'm Ramona Xuxa, and I studied your work on space propulsion systems while at M.I.T. I always saw pictures of you but never thought I would get to meet you. And if I say so myself, it's an honor meeting you, Dr. Collins," she gushed, extending her hand. "Your theories have helped revolutionize how we perceive space travel."

Shaking her hand, he replied, "The honor is genuinely mine," he said, a hint of warmth in his voice. "It's rare these days to encounter someone so enthusiastic about my research."

"Believe me, Doctor—" she began to gush again.

Tucker cleared his throat, pulling Ramona back from her moment of starstruck admiration, aware that she was veering into full fan-girl mode.

"Excuse me, Dr. Collins," she redirected the conversation. "This is Agent Dante Tucker of the CIA, along with Agent Smith, Agent Zingler, Agent McDowell and Agent Fernandez," gesturing to Edge Trident, Doom, and Pitch, respectively.

"Yes," he answered. "I am already aware of your visit,"

"How's that doctor?" Edge asked.

"I happened to be in the director's office when the guard buzzed him about your arrival," he explained, adjusting his glasses. "He was tied up at the moment, so I offered to escort you. This way, the director can prepare to receive you properly.

Now, if everyone is ready, we can move along," he added, gesturing toward a paved path that wound between the second and third buildings.

"So exactly how do you know Dr. Collins again?" Tucker asked Ramona as Dr. Collins guided the group down the pathway, with Trident, Doom, and Pitch at the rear.

"From studying propulsion technology, particularly space propulsion. He's the go-to guy for it," she answered.

"Where were you when I needed an introduction for my seminars," Dr. Collins laughed.

"I was probably still doing my time at NASA," she answered with a smile.

"NASA? That's great," he congratulated.

"So, Dr. Collins, may I ask what your role is here at the facility?" Edge chimed in.

Tucker appeared lost in thought, his mind tangled in Ramona's past, leaving little room to steer the discussion elsewhere. If they didn't reign in the topic soon, the conversation would inevitably drift toward Klingon Warbirds and their fictional battles.

"As Agent Xuxa stated, my expertise is in advanced propulsion, which helps me take on various roles here. One of them is as head of the propulsion laboratories, however the director has also blessed me with," he gave a pretended cough, "other duties as well, such as having oversight of manufacturing, a job I'm still getting accustomed to. Now may I ask you, what brings the CIA here?"

In the rear, some distance back, Pitch asked Trident, "So what do ya think about Agent Ramona?"

"I'm thinking she's hot," Trident answered.

"Yeah, for sure, but I'm wondering more about how she fits

into all this."

"I know what you mean. She seems fairly down to earth; a lot different from most spooks. A lot more so than Mr. Rigid Tucker."

"Yeah, but it bothers me that she comes to this random place, and the first bigwig we meet is an old acquaintance. Come on now; this Dr. Collins heads all the space technology in the world? It's too coincidental for my liking," Pitch continued.

"Your liking? When did you start have a liking? And what does that even mean?" Trident joked.

"Doom, would you let this fool borrow some of your reasoning?" Pitch requested.

Doom spoke slowly, each word carefully chosen as if they held great significance. "What I understand is that Edge chose to collaborate with her and Tucker on whatever this situation involves, and that's good enough for me to place my trust in them."

"Huh. I don't even know why I asked you," Pitch said.

"By the way, what type of name is Agent Zingler?" Trident complained, causing Doom to crack a random smile. Pitch just gave his *'you're an idiot'* look as they continued to follow the pack on the path ahead of them.

As the team walked down a pathway between storage buildings two and three, they were finally able to fully grasp the magnitude of the structures.

At the end of the paved path, a gray, tubular structure loomed, its domed roof reminiscent of an oversized bullet. The word "Mulch" sprawled across its surface in bold black letters. A solitary door, wide enough for a person to pass through, stood at its base. Dr. Collins retrieved his key card from around his neck and swiped it in front of a magnetic reader affixed to the door. A sharp beep sliced through the air as the lock clicked open. He pushed the door, and the hinges squeaked in protest, echoing softly inside.

Inside, the tubular corridor stretched about fifty feet, revealing a smooth concrete floor that gleamed under fluorescent lights. On either side, twin staircases spiraled down, their metal railings cool to the touch, leading to a polished door that stood like a sentinel at the end, complete with its own sleek card reader waiting for access.

As they stepped off the last stair, Dr. Collins remarked, "For your findings, Agent Xuxa, please note that our entrance security is derived from Titan II missile silo designs, updated with enhanced presence-detection and intrusion defense technology."

"Yes," said Ramona, "I reviewed the building plans."

"Then you're aware that just beyond this door lies our security checkpoint. Your credentials will be verified, and I anticipate no issues since the director has been informed of your arrival. However, your team will need to relinquish their weapons."

Doom murmured to Pitch, "Saw that coming."

"Ain't that the truth," Pitch responded under his breath.

"No, that will not happen," Ramona calmly informed Dr. Collins.

"I'm sorry, but it's site policy; no exceptions," Collins returned politely.

"Doctor, my men and I are here for a reason; relinquishing our weapons is out of the question," Edge said firmly.

"And what might that reason be?" Collins asked, stiffening his spine.

"That, Dr. Collins, is not your concern," Ramona respectfully informed him. "Please be assured that my authority extends to superseding your local security protocols if I deem it appropriate. And I do," she assured him gently while leaving no doubt that there was an iron hand inside the velvet glove.

"Okay. Well, I can see some difficulties here. It's probably better that I go first and see what I can do," Collins conceded, showing concern.

Tucker listened to the back-and-forth between Dr. Collins and Ramona, noting her commanding presence. While authority was crucial in their line of work, he found it surprising to witness her assertiveness, though he certainly appreciated it.

Collins seemed taken aback, perhaps mistaking her earlier enthusiasm for naivety. He pushed the door open and guided the team into the security checkpoint.

Upon entering, they found themselves in a cramped space dominated by a gleaming metal detector. To the left, a conveyor belt snaked along the wall, ready to process their belongings. On the right, a small nook offered just enough room for six people to stand shoulder to shoulder. A thick, bulletproof window stretched across the left side, providing a view into a semi-enclosed area where a guard stood, arms crossed and watchful. Beyond the glass, an access door connected to the guard booth, while directly ahead loomed a formidable door that marked the entrance to the complex beyond.

"Hold on a moment," Collins instructed, gesturing for them to stay back from the scanner.

As the entrance door clicked shut, a palpable sense of isolation enveloped them, reminiscent of an air lock sealing off the outside world. Behind the glass partition, three guards stood at attention, clad in gray fatigues and black vests, their eyes scanning the newcomers. Collins stepped through the metal detector, the device beeping softly as he passed, then made his way to the guard station at the far end of the booth. He lifted the handset, his voice low and urgent as he communicated with the seated guard. Moments later, the guard nodded and signaled to a colleague, who emerged from the booth and positioned himself a few feet away from Collins, arms crossed and watchful.

The team stood in silence, eyes fixed on the guarded booth. They exchanged glances, straining to catch snippets of the hushed conversation, but the words remained shrouded behind the metal detector's hum. Tension thickened the air as they observed the subtle shifts in the guards' body language, an unspoken communication that heightened their anticipation.

"Hey bud, can you tune into their frequency?" Edge asked.

"Not a problem," Doom replied moving to the front to relay the exchange. "The guards are telling the Doc that we cannot enter the facility armed, and Collins is trying to convince them that we've got the clout to override policy, but they're holding fast, still denying us entrance."

"You can read lips?" Tucker asked, directing his question to Doom, who did not respond to the question.

"He also makes a killer soufflé," Edge said, placing a hand on Doom's shoulder. "Yeah, he'll tell us what they're saying—," before he could finish his statement Ramona had stormed off through the detectors, causing them to squeal to life. She stopped at Collins' side.

"Or she'll tell us," Edge amended.

The guard next to Collins whipped up his gun. "Ma'am' stay behind the detectors until I give you permission to enter," he snapped. Even as the guard was raising his weapon, Tucker went for his gun, but a monster of a hand grabbed him from behind.

"You do that, she gets killed," Doom whispered. Tucker couldn't tell if it was the quiet, gravelly tone or the hulking hand that nearly crushed his bones like a twig, but he quickly saw the wisdom of Doom's advice.

Collins stepped between the guard and Ramona with his hand up and suggested to the guard inside, "Why don't we call Mr. Quinn and ask him to decide. I'm sure we wouldn't want to cause any unfortunate incidents here just on our own authority." The guard hesitated. "You always have your little green button," Collins added, nodding towards the guard's console.

The guard reluctantly lowered his weapon, his tone brusque as he directed Ramona, "Ma'am, please step back behind the detectors while you wait." The lack of politeness in his voice was unmistakable.

"So, what's the little green button?" Ramona asked as Collins escorted her back to the group.

"In the case of an aggressive breach, security has orders to initiate a lockdown, filling this very space with Etrophine. I'm not sure if you're familiar with the substance, but—"

"It's an incapacitating gas that will render us all unconscious in a matter of seconds," Ramona finished.

"That's correct. So, you can see why it's wiser not to yank their chain too vigorously," Collins said as if confiding a secret. "Just a moment more, and we'll have this all sorted out," the doctor said with an upbeat tone, as if he were diffusing tension at a social gathering.

After a brief pause, the guard stationed in the security room spoke through the intercom, "Dr. Collins, you and your team are cleared to proceed. Doctor, please escort them directly to their designated area." The team exchanged puzzled glances, their hands hovering near their holstered weapons. "You may keep your firearms," the guard added, his voice dripping with reluctance, as if he were forced to swallow a bitter pill.

"Well, that was interesting. Shall we?" Collins asked as he started towards the end door. As they strode by the guard booth, Edge's team caught the eyes of the men stationed within. A silent understanding passed between them, thick with unspoken tension and mutual distrust.

A heavy thud echoed through the chamber, followed by a sharp clack as the seal was broken. With a hiss, the door swung open on hydraulic hinges, revealing its imposing bulk. Four feet of reinforced concrete, sheathed in layers of titanium and stainless steel, loomed before them. Weighing over four tons, it was embedded deep within walls of the same formidable thickness, a barrier that defied brute strength.

"Again, as in a missile silo, a blast-proof door designed to withstand a nuclear detonation," said Collins, returning to tour-guide mode.

The team navigated a steeply sloped corridor, its ceiling crisscrossed with a tangle of pipes and wires. The only sound breaking the silence was the soft whoosh of air circulating through the ventilation system, punctuated by the muted thuds of their shoes against the cold concrete floor.

"This place is wild," "Wow," Pitch exclaimed in awe from the back of the group.

"Yeah, with this type of secrecy you would think we were heading into Area 51 or something," Trident responded.

"I know."

Tucker and Edge trailed closely behind Ramona and Dr. Collins.

"Doctor," Edge began, "with a manufacturing operation down here, how do you conceal the heat signature the facility must be giving off?"

"Excellent question, and you're absolutely correct," Dr. Collins began, his eyes glinting with enthusiasm. "This facility indeed emits a significant heat signature, especially given its remote location, which could easily attract unwanted scrutiny. This is where the lumberyard plays a crucial role. Did you happen to notice the large structure positioned behind the silo? That building serves as a kiln designed to expedite the drying process of lumber far more efficiently than traditional air drying methods. The kiln operates at a fluctuating temperature, allowing it to blend seamlessly with the facility's heat output, making it exceedingly challenging for any observer to pinpoint an additional source contributing to the warmth."

"Smart," Edge replied.

"I would have to agree with you," Dr. Collins replied. "Not to brag, but it was my suggestion. Sometimes the simplest ideas solve the largest problems."

As they approached the end of the corridor, Edge and his team lingered several paces behind Collins, Tucker, and Ramona. Collins flashed his badge at the card reader, then took a step back, lifting his arms theatrically as he declared, "Open sesame!" The sound of a mechanical click echoed through the air just before the door swung open.

Tucker and Ramona chuckled slightly, the right audience for his humor.

"The vibe so far hasn't exactly been welcoming," said Trident to the team, out of earshot of the other three.

"Wait 'til the rest of the guests arrive," replied Edge.

****

Collins ushered them through the door into a cramped lobby. Along the walls, there were a few chairs for six to eight people, and at the far end stood an unmanned reception desk. Tucker glanced at the vacant receptionist chair before turning to Collins, his eyebrows raised in question.

"If we'd known further in advance you were coming," explained their host, "we'd have put on the dog a little more, but we didn't have time to get the ceremonial touches in place. So, you will see the place in its day-to-day drone mode."

"Probably be more informative that way," replied Tucker.

They walked through the lobby and turned left down a narrow corridor, halting before an imposing mahogany door emblazoned with the name *Randolph Quinn, Facility Director* in bold letters. While not overly decorative, the door exuded a sense of executive sophistication that sharply contrasted with the stark, functional design of the surrounding facility.

"Well, this is where my part of the tour ends. Mr. Quinn will take over from here," said Collins, adjusting the glasses on his nose. "I must get back to managing. No matter how organized we get, the place still doesn't seem to run itself," he said, "other than into the ground."

"We appreciate your time and especially your, um, diplomacy, Dr. Collins. I hope to see you again as we tour," Ramona thanked him.

"I do hope so," replied Dr. Collins, giving a polite smile. "Gentleman, it was an experience meeting you," he said.

"The pleasure is all ours," answered Tucker.

Collins rapped his knuckles against the polished mahogany door, then swung it open with a flourish. "Director, your guests have arrived," he announced, his voice carrying a hint of excitement. He gestured toward the group with an inviting sweep of his arm. "Please, step inside."

Edge gestured for Pitch and Trident to stay by the door. They instantly fell into alert stances, their eyes scanning the corridor as the rest of the team moved past them. Collins shot a quick glance their way, tipping his head in acknowledgment. "Gentlemen," he murmured before striding toward a door labeled "Laboratories."

The Director's office sprawled with a warm glow, its wood-paneled walls exuding a sense of authority. Beneath their feet, a plush gray carpet muffled footsteps, inviting comfort. The rear wall gently arched, while the side walls showcased nine sleek HD flat panel displays, meticulously arranged in a video wall that angled toward the imposing desk at the center.

The Director's desk dominated the room, its curved front edge inviting attention. A section of the desktop hinged upward, revealing a series of tablet-sized displays that glowed softly, awaiting commands. Behind the desk, an LCD glass window stretched across the wall, currently opaque, concealing the sprawling facility beyond. Six plush conference chairs were arranged in an orderly fashion: two in front and four behind, creating a subtle tiered effect that positioned the Director as the focal point of this executive amphitheater.

As they stepped into the office, the Director stood, his hand slicing through the air in a swift greeting. The desktop displays retracted smoothly, folding away into the polished panels, transforming the desk into a sleek, uninterrupted surface. In the glass wall's reflection, Edge caught a glimpse of the screens as they shifted, revealing live feeds from various surveillance cameras throughout the facility.

Randolph Quinn towered at just over six feet, his physique lean and meticulously groomed. Clad in a suit that mirrored the sophistication of his office, he moved with the assured grace of a man well-versed in authority.

"Agent Xuxa, welcome to our facility. What can I do to help you?" Quinn greeted.

"Director Quinn, thank you for seeing us. This is Agent Dante Tucker, Agent Smith, and Agent McDowell, my colleagues from the CIA."

"It's a pleasure," he replied, shaking hands with each in turn, "but weren't there two more of you?"

"I have Agents Zingler and Fernandez standing guard outside the office. Please don't be offended but we are operating on high alert," Edge explained.

"I'd hope your experience with our security personnel would leave you feeling a little more comfortable now that you're on the inside," Quinn said.

Edge smiled. "Nonetheless..."

Quinn nodded. "Well, at least, allow me to give you the scenic part of the tour first," he said, gesturing to the displays on the side walls. On one side was a view of the forest through which they had just come. On the other was a fairly close view, obviously using a long-range telephoto lens, of the nest of a bald eagle with the male standing tall.

Quinn gestured to the national bird. "You can see all the pictures and videos of them you want, but it's only when you see them in real life that you realize how magnificent they are and why they are our national symbol."

"Seems like a lot of money to do bird watching," Doom vocalized.

"Oh, believe me, all this equipment is used mostly for business. The two cameras are supplemental surveillance that we only use for certain activities, and the displays are used for video conferencing. Still, every once in a while, I need to get a glimpse of the outside world to get over feeling like a coal miner," Quinn stated, self-deprecatingly. "My brother served on missile subs for years; I don't know how he did it."

"All you need is a video game system," Edge concluded.

"What's your choice of console?" Quinn grinned.

"I'm a HALO man, myself," replied Edge. Tucker struggled to maintain his composure, the unintended innuendo tugging at the corners of his mouth as he fought against a grin.

"Well then, if the day goes well maybe, we can do a mission later on," Quinn suggested.

"I'll prepare myself," Edge promised, glancing at Doom, who was barely concealing a smile.

"Please, have a seat," Quinn said, gesturing to the chairs. Tucker and Ramona sat in the two front chairs; Edge and Doom pulled chairs up next to them.

"Director, we've come to assess the status of your operations," Ramona began, "especially regarding your security measures.."

""I sensed this was a serious matter, particularly following the incident with the guards at the entrance. Their response should reassure you that we maintain a highly secure operation," he reiterated, echoing his earlier statement.

"Guards at the gate are only part of the equation," said Tucker. "We also need to look at record keeping, proper authorizations for access, and appropriate measures to protect restricted materials in transit."

"He's right, Director,' continued Ramona. "As you may have heard, around three forty-five PM on June thirtieth, an assault occurred in downtown Miami, targeting both Miami International Airport and the Turkey Point nuclear power plant by unidentified individuals."

"So, what does this have to do with me or my facility?" Quinn questioned.

"Your research into weaponizing AM-P technology," Ramona answered, frankly. "More precisely, the AM-P/B missile currently in development and production at this facility. Recent intelligence suggests that six missiles of this particular model were deployed during the assault."

"Agent Xuxa, as Mr. Tucker has correctly indicated, proper authorizations for access are required," Quinn replied. "I know you have presented your credentials, but we are still in the process of vetting them. Until I receive adequate confirmation that you are who you say you are and are authorized to make the inquiries you are making, I cannot allow you to go forward."

"Director, I can assure you that our clearances are genuine. The letter I presented contains identification codes that can be validated in seconds. Just to establish the full scope of why we're here, we are cleared not only regarding AM-P/B research and manufacturing but anything that may connect to Miami. Please do not make this harder than it has to be," Ramona countered.

"All the codes in your letter did indeed check out," Quinn acknowledged, "but given the nature of your inquiries I have taken the extra step of requesting a validation by a cognizant third party to be given directly to me by secure voice line. I have not yet received that, and it has taken longer than I expected, which does cause me some concern," Quinn finished, somewhat darkly.

"Exactly who is this third party?" Ramona demanded.

"Someone at the CIA in a position to know. I will not identify the person further," Quinn answered.

"But you do admit you're responsible for the AM-P/B missiles," Tucker chimed in.

"Mr. Tucker, I should that think we both have enough experience with this kind of situation to know that I can neither confirm nor deny any aspect of such things, including whether or not they even exist," replied Quinn, reproachfully.

The stillness in the room stretched uncomfortably until a sharp chime interrupted the tension, accompanied by a blinking red light on the wall. Quinn rose abruptly, his posture shifting from relaxed to alert.

"Please excuse me," he said, striding toward the blinking light. He presented his ID, and a hidden door across from the main entrance slid open with a soft hiss. The heavy door hinted at the soundproof chamber beyond, isolating whatever occurred inside from the outer world. Moments later, he reappeared, a satisfied grin spreading across his face. "That's one more complication resolved. Agent Xuxa, Agent Tucker, your clearances have been thoroughly validated, and I'm here to assist you. If you could just grant me a moment to prepare everything."

He reached into a desk drawer and took out a tablet.

"We should begin with a quick overview of the facility," he said, making a few taps on the screen.

Ramona was poised to mention her knowledge of the blueprints when the window behind Quinn's desk suddenly shifted to a clear view.

"*Wow,*" she thought. "*Quinn's right; the real thing is a lot more impressive than the pictures.*"

Before them loomed a vast cylindrical chamber, stretching a hundred yards across and soaring two stories high. The domed ceiling arched gracefully, supported by massive steel beams that glinted under the harsh lights. Below, the manufacturing floor rose twenty feet, bustling with activity, while the upper level, set back around the perimeter, housed offices and laboratories, its twelve-foot height creating an air of efficiency. At the center of the ceiling, a large octagonal control room hovered, where operators deftly maneuvered cranes and robotic trams, orchestrating the movement of materials and components. Catwalks crisscrossed from the control room's corners to the second level, while sturdy staircases descended to the busy manufacturing floor below.

"It's not the largest manufacturing floor ever," said Quinn, "but carving it out of solid rock is expensive, and even Uncle Sam needs to be as frugal as possible these days, so efficient use of space is critical. The circular shape helps by minimizing distances between the stages of production."

"Shipping and receiving is situated in the far-right corner, where incoming parts and materials are initially stored. From there, items progress to Detail Parts Manufacturing and Sub-assemblies on the near right. They then proceed to Airframe Final Assembly at the far end, followed by Electronics Integration on the near left. The final stages involve Software Installation and System Testing, also on the left. Once completed, products are transferred to secure storage directly across from us before heading out through the loading dock. In fact, a shipment is currently being loaded; you can spot the trailer by the overhead door."

"I want that truck held until I can inventory it," Edge pressed.

"It's not due to leave for a while yet," said Quinn, "but its departure window is not especially flexible. Anti-hijacking monitoring systems will expect to see it in transit along a defined route according to a very specific timetable. Otherwise, alarms will be set off, and that will get us into a pile of business that we will all be much happier without."

"It looks like a trailer full of wood from here," said Doom.

"Old bootlegger's trick," replied Quinn. "The shipping containers for the missiles fit inside an outer layer of boards. As far as anyone can tell, it's just a load of lumber."

Doom's face acknowledged the cleverness, but he asked, "How do they manage to slip past the weigh stations?"

"The drivers have special credentials that enable them to proceed without detailed scrutiny."

"Ever get hassled anyway?" Doom asked.

"Once. Some local hero decided he was too important to be kept in the dark and pressed farther than he should have. He quickly received a visit from some people who informed him of the error of his ways in a not especially subtle manner."

"What happened to him?" Doom continued.

"Oh, after they finished talking to him, they let him go home to change his shorts. He hasn't been a problem since," Quinn answered, a smile pulling at the corner of his lips.

A door at the back of the office clicked open, revealing a man clad in gray fatigues and a black vest, similar to the guards at the entrance. His collar gleamed with insignia, hinting at a higher rank.

"Allow me to introduce Captain Miller, Chief of our security unit. Captain, I'd like you to meet Agents Xuxa and Tucker of the CIA and Agents Smith and McDowell," Quinn introduced.

Remaining silent, the captain nodded in acknowledgment.

"So, where would you like to begin?" Quinn said giving them his attention once more.

"Your missile storage area, along with your inventory and

transport documentation," Edge answered.

While Ramona simultaneously, demanded, "Your testing lab, test scripts, and collected data."

"Very well: two teams in parallel," said Quinn. "Captain Miller, would you escort Agent Xuxa to the labs. Call Dr. Wright and make sure she will provide all the necessary data."

Quinn turned to Edge. "I'll escort you to the vault where we store the missiles, and you can examine our records at length."

"Thank you," Edge replied.

As they stepped out of the Director's office, Trident and Pitch remained stationed like silent sentinels, their eyes scanning the corridor.

"Director, Captain Miller," said Ramona, "this is Agent Zingler and Agent Fernandez," she introduced, gesturing at Trident and Pitch, respectively.

"Nice to meet you, gentlemen," Miller said, unconvincingly, as he walked away.

"That guy related to you?" Pitch said, noticing Millier's the lack of sociability.

"Wife's side maybe," Doom replied with a shrug.

"Agent Tucker, Agent Zingler, please accompany Agent Xuxa. Agents Fernandez and McDowell, you're with me," Edge directed.

The six agents split into two distinct groups, each team forming a tight circle as they prepared to move out.

"Very well," Quinn replied, glancing at Captain Miller, whose expression clearly betrayed his disdain for the task at hand.

"I'll call the doctor and have her meet us there. Follow me," Miller said brusquely as he walked away. Tucker caught a low murmur from the old man, the words laced with irritation as he muttered something unflattering about Quinn.

"Yay. We get mister smiles," Trident said to Tucker as they followed.

"I'd take him over Quinn," Tucker quipped.

As Edge's group trailed Quinn down a narrow corridor, a figure from Quinn's security unit slipped in behind them. He kept his distance, eyes scanning the surroundings while remaining out of earshot. Pitch observed the newcomer: a man in his late twenties, with smooth, dark skin and a gleaming bald head. The resemblance to a younger Dust struck him, though this man's face was softer, rounder, giving him an air of youthful vigilance.

The man's name tag read *RICE*.

Chapter 13

Brent, the guard, sighed heavily. The credentials checked out and indeed it was Keeast at the door.

"Great! Twice in one day I have to deal with these morons who think they're too cool for school. If I pushed the alarm button and gassed the bastard, I wonder if I could convince the boss, it was just a wrist cramp, and I didn't mean it?"

After a moment of hesitation, he finally pressed the button that unlocked the entrance door.

Keeast stood in the doorway, hands buried deep in the pockets of his sleek black tactical jacket, his head tilted slightly as he surveyed the guard with a sharp gaze. The absence of his polished business suit was striking; instead, he exuded an air of authority in fitted combat attire that hugged his form. Flanking him were three men, equally imposing in their matching gear, their eyes scanning the surroundings with a readiness that hinted at a mission.

"Tactical gear? I'm positive I saw him wearing a suit as he came down the corridor!" Brent thought, before he turned to replay the surveillance video on a side monitor and said quietly, "Heads up you to," he said to the other two guards in the both, Adams and Cooper.

The replay, which usually loaded without delay, chose this

moment to flash a message across the screen: Please wait.

Brent forced as amiable a tone as he could and said, "Good afternoon, sir. As always, kindly place any items you're carrying and the contents of your pockets onto the conveyor belt for scanning."

Keeast observed the other two guards shift into their designated positions, their movements deliberately nonchalant, yet gave the impression of practice duty. "Mr. Brent, at this juncture, I believe I've demonstrated enough to warrant a bit of trust," he stated in a steady tone, his eyes narrowing slightly as he assessed the situation.

"In God we trust, sir; all others we scan," Brent replied.

"You may find your trust is misplaced, Mr. Brent, but you can take that up with him face-to-face in a minute," Keeast warned.

Keeast flicked his wrist sharply, and from the shadows, a lithe figure in black fatigues burst forth. With a fluid motion, the newcomer leaped over the scanners, landing gracefully before slamming a small box against the booth glass before hitting the ground in a crouch.

Crafted for the sole purpose of penetrating fortified glass, the device clung to the window with a unique epoxy adhesive. As soon as it made contact, a corrosive agent nestled within its core activated, eating away at the surface. Within moments, the once-impenetrable one-inch-thick glass succumbed, becoming as fragile as a standard pane.

Brent's hand slammed down on the security alarm button, his heart racing as he activated the gas release. The monitors erupted into chaos, red borders flashing ominously around each screen, but then the system abruptly fell silent. Panic surged through him as he pressed the button again, then a third time, but the response was dead. No alarms, no warnings—just an eerie stillness in the air.

"Shit! The alarm are down?" he shouted, panic in his voice.

As Brent frantically scanned for a way out, the device erupted with a deafening roar, shattering the window and sending shards raining into the booth. He instinctively raised his arms to shield his face, but sharp fragments embedded themselves in his skin, piercing his cheeks and blinding him with pain. A scream tore from his lips as he crumpled to the floor.

Adams, quick on his feet, darted forward, positioning himself between Brent and the jagged opening. With one hand, he dragged Brent away from the chaos, while his other hand kept his MP5 submachine gun aimed at the gaping hole, ready for any threat. Cooper, the lead guard, barked orders into his radio, rallying the rest of the security team to respond. He too focused on the shattered window, his weapon poised for action, eyes scanning for any sign of danger.

Hitoshi sat patiently, disdainfully brushing a small amount of glass from his clothes. As the architect of their recently updated security system, he had inserted a backdoor login that granted him complete access to the facility's security controls. With a portable device in hand, Hitoshi's fingers danced across the screen, and the massive main entrance door unlatched, beginning its ponderous opening.

Inside the security booth, Brent leaned against his partner, blood seeping from his wounds as he waited anxiously while Cooper scrambled to formulate a defensive plan. The only entrance or exit from the room was the heavily reinforced door leading into the lobby. The booth had been engineered to endure any conceivable assault. The protocol in the event of an attempted breach dictated that the guards would incapacitate the attackers with gas and hold their position until reinforcements arrived. A small weapons locker could have supplied them with an array of firearms and ammunition, but with the security system down, it remained locked tight.

With a few more taps Hitoshi had the guard's booth open with a click. At the same moment, two silver canisters soared through the shattered window and exploded in mid-air. The guards lacked the reaction time to shield themselves from the blinding flash-bangs, and they endured the full brunt of their effects.

The three men flanking Keeast burst through the doorway, their boots pounding against the floor as they veered sharply to the right. They quickly spotted Cooper sprawled on the ground, his body limp and unresponsive. Without hesitation, one of them raised his weapon and fired two shots into Cooper's chest, the deafening cracks echoing in the chaos, followed by a final shot that struck him in the head, silencing any remnant of life.

Meanwhile, the others split off, one veering left while the other advanced toward the center. They moved with purpose, their eyes locked on Brent and Adams, who were crouched low, adrenaline coursing through their veins as they braced for the impending confrontation. The intruders loomed over them, ready to unleash the next wave of violence.

With the guard's booth now unlocked, Hitoshi redirected his attention to the lobby. Within moments, he manipulated the controls, and the entrance door swung open, granting access to Keeast's squad. They surged forward, each step echoing the urgency of their mission.

Battered and bruised, the two guards braced themselves, acutely aware that their time was running out. As the disorienting effects of the flash-bang faded, Brent felt the searing pain return, sharp and relentless. The echo of footfalls reached his ears—heavy, deliberate, and multiplying. He counted at least three times the number of intruders he had glimpsed with Keeast just before the chaos erupted. Each step resonated ominously, a countdown to their impending doom.

"This fucker hacked the whole damn system and blinded us. He must have planned this from day one," Brent realized. He heard the slow, calculated footsteps of a single man entering the room, each step crunching on the shards of broken glass beneath his feet.

"Not him," Brent grunted in pain, recognizing the methodical steps: "Keeast."

"The one and only," Keeast said, as his men in the room picked up Adams. "Remember no loose ends," Keeast gestured to one of his men. "We must show them what happens to people who are not my friends."

The metallic rasp of a blade sliding from its sheath sliced through the air, quickly followed by a sickening sound as it met flesh, punctuated by a drawn-out gasp that echoed in the chaos. Brent's body went cold, a shiver racing down his spine as he registered the brutal reality of his friend's murder.

"Ah, so this is the clown who always gives me those warm welcomes," Keeast sneered as his men lifted Brent to his feet. "Damn, you have glass in your eyes!" Keeast teased. "But then again, you've been in the dark this entire time, perceiving only the illusions that Mr. Hitoshi has crafted for you. If you're truly blind, how can you possibly grasp the delight I'm about to take in ending your life?"

Once more, he signaled to one of his men, who swiftly plunged his knife beneath the guard's ribcage, driving it deep into his heart. As the warmth of life ebbed away, Brent managed to form a smile, a flicker of defiance lighting up his fading consciousness. Even in this final moment, he found solace in the thought that he would continue to vex the bastard, even from beyond the grave.

****

Rubbing his eyes, Trident felt an unsettling restlessness creep in. He had already surveyed the lab, mapping out potential defensive and offensive positions, while counting the ceiling tiles for the second time. The soft glow of the lab's lights caught him off guard, a stark contrast to the unforgiving glare of the manufacturing dungeon he had come to despise.

The lab sprawled into two distinct sections, separated by a wide aisle that led to entry and exit doors at either end. To the left, expansive rooms dominated the space. The first was a pristine clean room, flanked by antechambers where workers donned white full-body suits, evoking images of villains from classic sci-fi flicks. At the far end, the server room buzzed with life, filled with towering racks of blinking computers and humming communication equipment. On the right side, two areas stood marked by bold signs: one read *Operating System & Navigation*, while the other declared *Targeting and Activation*.

From what he overheard, this was where the software was developed. In each area, cubicles containing powerful workstations surrounded a group of workbenches. Oscilloscopes and other test equipment hung from overhead racks while the workbenches were filled with electronic components and assemblies that sometimes spilled over onto the floor.

"Too bad Pitch didn't get assigned here," Trident thought. *"This is a geek's Christmas."*

Driven by curiosity, he approached a door that had previously escaped his notice, pondering where it might lead. A grunt from his side caught his attention, and he turned to see one of the guards gripping his MP5 with a white-knuckled intensity, shaking his head in warning. The gesture halted Trident's exploration abruptly. He despised uncertainty; for a fleeting moment, he considered asking Ramona to override the guard's authority, allowing him to sneak a glance behind the door. However, he noticed her engrossed in a discussion with lab personnel, her focus unwavering. Deciding against it, he retraced his steps, returning to the table where the others had gathered.

Trident glanced at Tucker, who leaned forward, his eyes fixed on Ramona and the scientists. He strained to catch snippets of their discussion, but without his specs, the rapid shifts in topics eluded him. One moment, the group delved into the intricacies of designing hardware robust enough to withstand violent impacts and relentless vibrations. In the next breath, they shifted to the frustrating software glitches that had caused missiles to activate unexpectedly mid-flight.

Out of the corner of his eye, Trident spotted Miller making his way toward him. There was an unmistakable authority in the older man's stride, a quiet confidence that set him apart from the rest. It wasn't just the streaks of gray in his hair or the way he surveyed the younger soldiers with a knowing gaze. It was the weight of experience that hung around him like a well-worn cloak. Unlike, the guard detail which consisted of young soldiers, all in their mid-twenties to early thirties, their eager faces betraying a lack of real-world combat experience—Trident could almost picture them hunched over game consoles, fingers dancing over controllers in a digital battlefield.

"You understand what they're talking about?" Captain Miller inquired, his tone devoid of genuine curiosity, instead serving as a tactic to draw Trident's focus.

"I got lost after they said, 'This is where we work on the guidance system.'" Trident replied, attempting to lighten the mood, though it was a challenge given the way the man's expression seemed frozen in a decade-long frown.

"So then why are you here? What is the *real* purpose of this visit?" he snapped, making it clear that this was not a conversation but an interrogation.

"Like I said we're here to..." Trident tried to respond but was cut off.

"Put the canned response back in the can, son," Miller said as he glared at Trident.

"All due respect, sir, but I am not authorized to disclose any details of our visit. You will have to speak to Agent Tucker or Agent Xuxa," Trident replied, apologetically.

Miller's gaze remained fixed on Trident, his brow furrowing as he assessed the younger man. The tension in the air thickened, an unspoken question hovering between them. Trident could feel the weight of Miller's scrutiny, as if the captain were weighing his worth against an invisible scale. A flicker of uncertainty crossed Miller's features, and for a moment, it seemed he wrestled with the decision to confide in someone outside his usual circle. Then, as if a switch had been flipped, resolve settled onto his face, signaling that he had reached a conclusion.

"Agent Zingler, if that is your name," he began, "we only get inspected three times a year, always by the same men, also CIA. Their "inspections" don't amount to more than sight-seeing, and they sure don't dig into the details the way Agent Xuxa over there is doing. They only want to know how many missiles are complete and why it isn't more," Miller said before he continued. "The atmosphere around here since Miami has been downright psychotic. I will bet my ever so generous government retirement plan that: one, they are connected to it and, two, you are here to find out who they are."

Trident made another attempt to interject, but as he opened his mouth, Captain Miller abruptly averted his gaze and raised a hand to his ear. In unison, the other security officers nearby mirrored his actions, their expressions shifting to grim concern. A message crackled through the radio, and the air seemed to become heavy as they absorbed the implications of the transmission.

Chapter 14

Quinn led Edge, Doom, and Pitch across the catwalk that spanned above the Detailed Parts and Sub-assembly station. Below them, the floor buzzed with activity, machines positioned in sweeping arcs that resembled the rings of a tree surrounding the central staircase. Towering water jets and laser cutters occupied the outer perimeter, their metallic surfaces gleaming under the harsh overhead lights, while smaller lathes and milling machines nestled closer to the center, their whirring and clanking sounds merging into a mechanical symphony.

Pathways crisscrossed the machine arcs like spokes on a wheel. Slim corridors extended outward from the center, allowing operators to access the machines, while wider routes branched from the outer edges, enabling robotic trams to transport materials and components between different workstations.

From the vantage point of Quinn's office, the manufacturing area unfolded at approximately the one o'clock mark on the floor. Here, an array of metal components in diverse sizes and shapes were crafted. As these parts progressed in a clockwise motion through the assembly stages, they gradually transformed into distinctly missile-shaped structures.

Quinn detailed the missile manufacturing process to Edge, meticulously outlining each step of construction. As Quinn's explanations stretched on, Edge's impatience grew palpable.

"Mr. Quinn," Edge interrupted. "Your manufacturing process is ingenious. However, my goal for the day is to conduct an audit of your production and shipping records."

"Of course," replied Quinn, "but first, you must grasp the entire process before delving into the records. Within those documents, you'll encounter mentions of missiles that are still in the early stages of assembly or merely exist as raw materials and components, some of which won't even enter production for several weeks. We all want to ensure the audit is precise, after all."

Edge acknowledged Quinn with a slight nod, but he countered. "I trust your systems can generate a report detailing each missile's manufacturing stage, completion percentage, and cost tracking value. I don't need precise locations on the shop floor, but I must inspect your vault and security measures. Additionally, I'm eager to review the cargo on that truck. You mentioned they're on a tight timeline, so we should act quickly.

"Very well," Quinn agreed, knowing he had lost that bit of verbal swordplay. "The truck is not scheduled to leave for some time yet so you will certainly have adequate opportunity to examine it. I was only making the point that holding it up would introduce unnecessary complications."

"Good to hear," said Edge, "but if you could move a bit quicker, I'd feel better."

"So be it," said Quinn, who proceeded to condense his tour, giving a quick overview of how the machinery for the facility had been purchased through a dummy company and trans-shipped here.

"If anyone was watching, wouldn't it seem strange to have all that machining equipment going into a lumber yard?" asked

Doom.

"Just as we hide outgoing shipments in lumber, we hide incoming ones the same way. The lumber yard offers endless ways to camouflage them," Quinn said with pride.

"You said 'use,'" Pitch noted. "Are you still bringing in machinery?"

"Now and then, but mostly to hide parts and materials. We can't afford anyone knowing we exist."

"What parts would you buy as opposed to making?" Edge asked

"Mostly advanced tech that's hard to build and needed in such small quantities, it's not worth setting up production here," Quinn explained.

"Is quality an issue, when you're required to use the lowest bidder?" Pitched asked.

"We operate under 'best value' rules, which let us choose quality over price—within reason. I'm surprised an auditor like you doesn't know that," Quinn said, his tone dripping with condescension, as if addressing an inept subordinate.

Pitch had frozen, fearing he had blown their cover—but Edge had cut in. "Agent Fernandez is on my team for his technical expertise. He's still learning the contractual side, so I expect you to treat any questions from him with proper respect."

"My apologies," said Quinn, meekly. He'd been dope-slapped by this guy twice in as many minutes, and it was starting to get under his skin.

By that time, they had arrived at the control room—an almost octagonal space, more like a square with its corners trimmed away to make room for doors leading to the catwalks. Along the main walls, operators sat at their consoles, closely monitoring the activity below.

"Here," Quinn said, "is the nerve center of the factory floor. Operators at the machines and assembly stations signal when they need parts or have completed components, and the robotic tram handles the transport. I know your main concern is security—especially the missile vault—so take a look at that monitor there."

He gestured toward a screen displaying two windows—one outlined in blinking yellow, the other in blinking red. "A blinking border signals a security issue that requires attention. Yellow means a vehicle is at the shipping and receiving dock. That red one," he added, pointing, "means the missile vault is currently open."

"Who has access to the vault?" Edge asked.

"Me, and a few key staff members," Quinn explained. "Mainly, it's the head of the shipping department who opens it. But anytime he needs access—whether to store missiles or prepare them for shipment—he has to notify the security desk first. They send an armed guard, who badges in both him and the shipper, acting like a co-signer. The guard also has to stay there the entire time the vault is open. It's the same kind of procedure as when a truck is at the dock—that's what the yellow-bordered window represents."

"Why aren't both alert levels red?" asked Doom.

"Severity level; having the truck on premises is not as big a concern as having the vault open," Quinn faced him.

"You've got a lot of guards patrolling," Doom remarked. "Add a few more, and this place might start looking more like a prison than a factory."

"Our main security concern is keeping intruders off the property—usually local kids, half-drunk and looking to prove something by climbing a fence," he said. "Inside, the guard presence is minimal—just a few stationed at restricted areas, others assigned as needed for specific tasks like monitoring the loading dock or the missile vault, and people like Mr. Rice, who are here to escort visitors."

"MP5s seem a little heavy duty for that." Edge commented.

"Normally, sidearms are enough," Quinn said, "but after what happened in Miami—and with some rumors floating around that we might be connected—we've decided to step things up a bit."

At that moment, Rice sprinted toward Quinn, urgency etched across his face. Quinn's phone shrieked with a sharp, piercing tone, slicing through the low hum of machinery. Out on the factory floor, guards were moving quickly, corralling workers into small, tight groups. Pitch glanced at Doom, eyebrows raised and jaw tight—no words needed.

Quinn glanced at his phone screen, his expression calm, almost indifferent. "Hmm," he said, as if commenting on the weather. "Looks like we've got an incident." He turned the phone so the others could see. Across the display, a message pulsed in bold red letters: **SEC LVL 1: BREACH.**

✱✱✱✱

Jasmine one of the many workers at the site, settled at the table, sharing a laugh with colleagues over a simple meal as they wrapped up their packing. Her eyes sparkled with exhaustion and satisfaction—a fresh glow after three months underground, living twenty-four seven in cramped quarters that felt more like a college dorm than luxury. Despite the spartan surroundings, she wore a smile that said she wouldn't trade it for anything.

Jasmine's diploma from Princeton—undergrad honors, plus

master's degrees in electrical engineering and computer science. When the job offer came through a company she'd applied to, her eyes lingered longer on the salary figure, but it was the project details—the cutting-edge work, the challenge—that truly lit a fire in her.

The schedule had been tough to adjust to at first. Spending three months beneath a mountain wore on everyone, so each weekend they took a group bus over an hour away to the nearest town for a brief break. After three months on the job, they earned three weeks away from it all. Jasmine counted the days until she could go home—though the thought of not being able to share a single detail of her work, locked away in secrecy, made the return feel oddly distant.

She couldn't help but chuckle at the word *secret*. Never in her life had she imagined working on a government project so classified she couldn't share a thing—funded by the government but wrapped in silence. This was a "Black" project, one so hidden even the government denied its existence. She'd even been handed a cover story to use whenever friends or family asked what she did.

She looked forward to her time above ground, savoring the thought of fresh air and open skies. Yet, beneath it all, her coworkers had become more than just colleagues—they were a community where she truly felt at home.

"Jasmine!? Hey, you totally spaced out on us again," Mike called out, snapping her back to the moment.

"Sorry, yeah, lost in thought again," She replied sheepishly.

Jasmine had known Mike since college—she was a freshman while he was wrapping up his doctorate. She'd always thought he was attractive, and sometimes caught hints that he felt the same. Getting involved with a coworker was off-limits, so she kept things playful, enjoying their teasing without crossing any lines.

"Please tell me you're not daydreaming about turbines again," he said, taking a bite of his sandwich. "You're the only girl I know who actually gets lost in thoughts about those things."

"What can I say? Assembling one of those and hearing it come to life is just...incredible," she replied, letting the last word linger with a teasing, sultry edge.

"I don't know about you, but the only machine that makes me that happy is a lot smaller—and way better—than any turbine," Chelsea, another co-worker, quipped with a grin.

"Hey Mike, want my pickle? Somehow, it's lost its appeal after that comment," joked Steve, one of the facility's off-duty guards.

Mike shot him a grateful-but-no-thanks look and laughed.

The pressure to get the new prototype up and running had been intense, but they'd made the deadline. The tension that had hung over the team lately was finally easing, and Jasmine couldn't help but smile at the sight of everyone's relief and renewed spirits.

Steve was the only friend Jasmine had who didn't rely on stress relief. He'd dropped out of high school, enlisted in the army, and after five years in Iraq, landed a job as a security guard at the facility—nicknamed "Mount Uneventful" by the guards. While most of the guards kept to themselves, Steve was one of the rare few who actually hung out with the tech crew.

Mike glanced at his watch. "Alright, everyone, it's been a long haul, but we got it done. Now we've got a vacation waiting, and the longer we sit here, the less time we'll have out there," he said, standing up and heading toward his room.

"Hey man, I can't believe you're leaving me here with these two," Steve said, nodding toward Jasmine and Chelsea with a mock look of helplessness. "They're gonna start talking all 'techie smart,' and all I'll be able to do is just sit here and take it."

"Just bring up sports cars, and Jasmine will be packing her bags to go with you on vacation," Mike joked.

"Hey, I'm not that easy," she protested, as Mike winked and strolled away from the table.

The hallway door slid open with a smooth hiss, and the chatter in the room instantly died. Three armored figures stepped inside, weapons drawn and eyes scanning. Jasmine's gaze locked on them as they moved—like shadowy figures emerging from another world, their black armor and masked helmets stripping away any hint of humanity.

Time seemed to stop. Her mind blanked, unable to process what was happening—until her eyes landed on Mike sprawled on the floor. She hadn't even noticed the first soldier's gunfire—three sharp shots hitting his chest—nor the rising screams that echoed around her.

Steve's shout tore through the haze, jolting her back. "GET DOWN!" he yelled, but before the words fully registered, the second soldier's bullet slammed into his face, and he crumpled backward to the floor.

With a sharp cry, Chelsea snatched up her chair and hurled it at the soldier who'd just gunned down Steve. The impact hit squarely, jolting him back a step. Without hesitation, she grabbed Jasmine's arm and yanked her toward the opposite doorway. Jasmine stumbled after her, heart pounding, eyes sweeping the break room in fragments—colleagues scrambling behind tables, crawling for cover, some frozen in place. As they fled, Steve's radio, knocked loose and still on the floor, crackled to life in a frantic loop as someone yelled, *"Code one! Breach! It's Keeast! Code one! Breach! It's Keeast!"*

Jasmine's eyes locked onto the glowing red exit sign across the room. Her arm shot out, finger stabbing the air. "There!"

Chelsea was already moving. Jasmine's legs pumped like pistons, sneakers slapping the concrete as adrenaline surged. The door loomed closer—ten feet, maybe less.

Then came the impact.

A searing punch to her spine, then another, then two more—each one folding her body mid-stride. She hit the ground hard, cheek scraping against the cold floor, breath stolen from her lungs.

Her vision blurred.

Through the haze, she saw Chelsea twist violently, limbs flailing as crimson bursts erupted from her torso. The force hurled her sideways, her body crumpling like a marionette with its strings cut.

The Order moved like a machine—no hesitation, no wasted motion. Their rifles barked in rhythm, cutting down bodies whether they ran, crawled, or simply lay still.

A second wave of soldiers stormed in, boots pounding against tile and concrete. Without a word, the two teams split the living quarters like butchers dividing a carcass, sweeping through hallways and rooms with cold efficiency.

In one cramped dorm, a squad paused outside a closet door. Muffled whimpers leaked through the wood. One soldier yanked it open.

Inside, a handful of workers huddled together, knees drawn to chests, eyes wide and wet—like kids caught sneaking out after curfew.

The gunfire that followed was deafening.

When it stopped, the walls dripped red. The bodies slumped in a heap, riddled and ruined, the scene echoing the infamous carnage of Chicago's blood-soaked February.

Behind a wall of monitors, Hitoshi's fingers danced across the keyboard, his face lit by the glow of schematics and blinking alerts.

With a few keystrokes, hallway doors slid open for the Order's advance—silent, seamless. Moments later, others slammed shut with mechanical finality, trapping panicked workers inside labs and lounges.

Security teams scrambled, only to find their routes sealed, their fallback positions cut off. Every move the Order made was mirrored by Hitoshi's invisible hand, guiding them like pieces on a board. The facility wasn't just compromised—it was choreographed.

At the rear strode the deadliest of the demons. Keeast and Draggo moved with lazy confidence, eyes sweeping the carnage like connoisseurs. Keeast let a smile slip—everything was going exactly to plan.

Over the years, he'd built the perfect setup—crafted the work schedule, hired weak security, and handed Hitoshi the keys to the mainframe. The mission was stacked in their favor. Throwing in Tucker and his wild dog Pierce's was just icing.

A gasp from the next room snapped him out of his thoughts.

Blood smeared the tiles beneath her as a worker dragged herself forward, one arm trembling, the other limp. The bed loomed just ahead—her last hope. She clawed toward its shadow, breath hitching with each inch.

Boots thudded behind her.

Her heart surged. Maybe a guard. Maybe help.

She twisted her head.

A black-clad figure filled the doorway, as he smoothly lifted their rifle, and took aim.

Her lips parted in a fragile whimper, eyes wide with the kind of fear that begged for mercy but knew none was coming.

Time stretched, each heartbeat a thunderclap in her ears.

Then—voices. Sharp, clipped. An order barked.

The assassin hesitated, lowered his rifle, and turned away. She lay frozen, lungs burning, mind racing. Maybe they needed someone alive. Maybe she was worth keeping. Hope flickered, fragile and desperate, clinging to the silence he left behind.

The room dimmed as two more figures filled the doorway. One was massive—bear-like, brutal. The other, smaller, radiated a quiet, chilling menace. She knew then: death was no longer a possibility. It was a promise.

Keeast studied the woman, arms folded, a slow smile curling on his lips. Draggo caught the cue and stepped forward, fingers brushing the grip of his Desert Eagle. Keeast raised one hand, then tapped his hip. Draggo paused, let the gun sink back into its holster, and drew his survival knife instead—blackened steel gleaming under the harsh fluorescent lights. He admired its edge, then shifted his gaze to the trembling technician and began his approach. Keeast leaned into the doorframe, her pleading voice washing over him like a favorite song.

About the Author

Dameon Gibbs holds an BA in Anthropology and World History and an MA in Classical Studies. For the past five years he has worked with inner-city youth in Baltimore, Maryland. He has been an avid writer since his days in high school during the late 1990's. He enjoys the creative process of all writing genres, whether it be religious, poetic, science fiction, historical, biographies or action adventure.

Dameon is married to fellow author Tiffany Michele.

You can connect with me on:

- https://gibbspublishingconglomerate.com
- https://www.facebook.com/GibbsPublishing